DRAGON WARS

THE FLAMING FENCE

BOOK 17

D1739085

CRAIG HALLORAN

Dragon Wars: The Flaming Fence - Book 17

By Craig Halloran

★★★★★

Copyright © 2021 by Craig Halloran

Amazon Edition

TWO-TEN BOOK PRESS

PO Box 4215, Charleston, WV 25364

ISBN Paperback: 979-8-741077-52-8

ISBN Hardback: 978-1-946218-97-1

www.craighalloran.com

Publisher's Note

This book is a work of fiction. Names, characters, places, and incidents either are the product of the author's imagination or are used fictitiously, and any resemblance to actual persons, living or dead, events, or locales is entirely coincidental.

 Created with Vellum

1

STREAK BUMPED Zanna in the chest with his snout. He'd grown to be bigger than a middling dragon. His skull was armored with hard ridges, and a stout, well-developed horn stuck out from the end of his nose. "The great Zanna Paydark," he said as he shoved her back toward the ledge of the mountain camp. "What's the matter? Did you think you'd receive a warm welcome? A hug, perhaps?"

Zanna pushed back against his snout. With her hands on his horn, she said, "Stop acting like a child and tell me what you did with Grey Cloak and Dyphestive."

Streak continued to advance. His yellow eyes glowed, and his breath turned hot.

Her boots slid across the grass. "Will you listen to me?"

"I'll tell you what. Why don't you tell me where you've been all this time. Hm? That would be nice."

Her strength was feeble compared to his natural might. She slid back farther. Streak wasn't alone, either. Two ugly brutes with shaggy hair accompanied him. They were built like thick-limbed blacksmiths, though one was beefier than the other. They wore long winter coats. Their names were Chinns and Chubb, and they flanked Zanna, holding long walking sticks.

"I've been making sacrifices the same as the rest of us all these years." She pushed back. "You have to believe me, Streak."

"You don't look like you've suffered much to me. And that's a very vague answer." With a flip of his horn, he knocked Zanna off of the ledge. "Bye, now."

Chinns and Chubb rushed to the edge and leaned over.

"You really tossed her over," Chinns said in a rough but excited voice. "I didn't think you'd kill her."

"Oh, she'll be back." Streak walked toward the campfire. "Trust me. It will take more than a fall to kill her."

"What is that?" Chubb asked, pointing over the ledge.

Zanna rose from the darkness of the night. The Cloak of Legends had broken her fall, and she'd used her wizardry to guide her upward. She'd mastered the trick long ago. Zanna floated over Chinns and Chubb as their mouths gaped. Then she made a soft landing behind Streak. "We don't have time for games."

"Time? I've been squatting in the hills for season after

season, and you want to talk about time?" Streak studied her from the corner of his eye. "I don't think so."

Zanna sighed. She'd expected some pushback, but she hadn't expected her son and Dyphestive to be completely missing. "You need to trust me, Streak. I'm not the enemy here. Black Frost is. I've been gathering information about him and preparing for the next step."

"Yeah, yeah. You said that." He gazed into the flames. "I've given a lot of thought to much you've had to say."

Chinns and Chubb crept up behind Zanna.

She turned and said, "Come one step closer, and I'll send the both of you over the rim."

Whack! Streak's tail hit her square in the back and forced her flat on her face. With the wind knocked out of her, she rolled away, avoiding another swat of Streak's tail. It landed beside her, and snow flew up.

Chinns tackled Zanna. His large frame crushed her into the ground. She slid out of a headlock, hooked his arm, and hip-tossed him away. A wooden staff came out of nowhere and hit her head. Stars burst in her eyes, and the air hummed.

She caught Chubb's second swing with her hand. He yanked back, but she held the staff fast.

"You're going to regret this." She sent a charge of wizard fire into the staff, which exploded into splinters. Chubb jumped away, shouting and stuffing his singed hands into the snow.

Footsteps rushed in behind her. She drove the Rod of Weapons into Chinns's gut with a backward jab.

"Oof!" Chinns went down, clutching his solar plexus and gasping.

Streak was gone.

The fire in the Rod of Weapons ignited. "Streak, no more games. We need to talk about this like adults." She scanned the camp. "I don't want to hurt you."

A shadow descended like a bolt of black lightning. Silently, Streak glided into her and knocked her flat. Then he stood on top of her, crushing her body into the frosty ground.

"I've been waiting for the day you'd show up, Zanna. Planning what I would do and say." He sank his claws into the Cloak of Legends and started to pull it from her body. "This is for my friends." With his mouth, he ripped the Rod of Weapons from her grip and tossed it at Chinns's feet. "And so is this."

With her face in the icy dirt, she asked, "What do you want from me?"

"You are going to free my friends. Then you're going to walk away and never be heard from again."

"I can't do that." She spit snow from her mouth. "You need me."

"I'm not going to give you a choice." His chest scales started warm like coals. "You *will* leave, or you *will* die. Give me your word, Zanna!"

Streak started to crush her under his girth.

Her cheeks swelled, as if her head were about to pop. "I will," she gasped. "I swear it! I will!"

Streak backed off, flipped her onto her back, and stuck his nose into her face. "You'd better."

2

ZANNA RUBBED HER CHEST. With the Cloak of Legends removed, she was stripped down to a black shirt, trousers, a sword belt, a bandolier of vials, and other weapons. Wincing, she followed Streak behind the cabin that she and the blood brothers had built long ago.

The log building was in good order, and smoke puffed from the chimney.

Her teeth chattered. Without the Cloak of Legends to keep her warm, she had no way to fight off the bitter cold of the windy mountains.

Streak stopped behind the cabin, which butted against the hills. He breathed out a stream of flame, setting a pile of snow-buried logs on fire. "Get the shovels, boys. You have some digging to do."

"As you wish, Master Streak," they said.

Zanna warmed her hands over the fire. "How'd you come across them?"

"Led by a rotten brood, they stumbled into the hills a while back. I saved them, and they swore their loyalty and have been faithful ever since."

She blew into her hands. "Are you sure about that?"

"They could have left long ago, with a chest full of treasure, but they didn't. For some reason, they stayed."

"And you've been training them?"

"I didn't have anything else to do."

She nodded.

Chinns and Chubb returned, shovels in hand, and started digging into the hillside.

"It's frozen, Master. Gonna take some time," Chubb said.

"Stay back." Streak sent a stream of flame across the hillside. The frozen overgrowth burned, and smoke started to rise. "That will soften it."

Zanna squatted over the flames and asked, "So, you buried them, huh?"

Watching the brothers dig, Streak replied, "It makes a great hiding spot, and it's easier to recover them here than dumping them in a river like we did the Bedlam Brothers."

"A wise move. But did you ever stop to think what would happen if the spell wore off?"

"No."

"You'd better hope it didn't, or you might not find anything but skeletons in there."

Streak snorted out smoke and said, "I took my chances."

With frosty breath coming out of their mouths, Chinns and Chubb dug their shovels into the hillside and flipped scoopfuls over their shoulders. The dirt started to pile up. Then one of the shovels bit into stone.

"Careful," Streak warned them.

"I think we found them. It was a shallow grave, after all," Chubb said.

They cleared away the dirt from Dyphestive's brawny, hunched form.

The shocked expression on Dyphestive's stony face made Zanna's heart sink. She'd been in the same situation before. Being turned into stone was torment.

"He looks good—scared half to death but good," Chinns commented. He started digging out the figure beside Dyphestive. "This one's a little deeper, Master Streak. We'll have him cleared soon."

Zanna stood behind the men, watching over their shoulders. Walls of dirt fell away. The grit packed around Grey Cloak's face was brushed away and cleared. His eyebrows were knitted together, and anger burned in his expression. She felt his eyes looking right through her.

"I'm going to need my scroll," she said.

Streak flicked his pink tongue out and caught a

snowflake. "You mean that one that took a plethora of seasons to fetch from the Wizard Watch?"

"That's the one."

"I take it it's in the cloak." He lifted it over to her with his tail. "Make it quick."

She reached into the warm pockets of the cloak and removed the scroll. "That will do." The leather cord around the scroll was still intact. She loosened the string and started unrolling the parchment.

"This will work, won't it?" Streak asked.

"It will be my first attempt, but I'm confident it will." She eyed the statues. "It would be ideal if we could place them where it happened."

Streak glowered at her. "We've waited long enough. Make it happen."

Chinns and Chubb moved aside and leaned on their shovels.

Grey Cloak and Dyphestive's bodies were still half buried in the mountain, covered up to the knees.

Zanna moved forward and started to read silently. Scrolls were tricky devices. One slip of the tongue, and the entire spell could unravel. "See to it I have no distractions."

Streak nodded. "You won't."

She drew in a deep breath through her nose and started reading. Mystical words flowed from her lips like a river of honey. As she read each word, it radiated and vanished from the page. Her skin warmed. The scroll became a living thing in her hand. Power flowed from her mouth and carried across the icy air into Grey Cloak's and Dyphestive's bodies.

Grey Cloak existed in a sea of blackness, where no light or sound lived. Only his thoughts accompanied him. He was trapped in a dark abyss, with no avenue of escape. He had no sense of time or self. He couldn't feel heat or cold. His mind was a barren wasteland, where he wandered.

He relived every moment of his life he could recall, agonizing over every mistake he'd ever made. The worst of all had been trusting his mother, who'd turned him to stone. He relived the moment a thousand times. He'd sat by the campfire, eating and laughing, then made a decision to let Zanna have her way. Then his tongue thickened, and his body turned as rigid as a board. He saw the look of betrayal in her eyes. It left a lasting, burning impression he would never forget.

I know what she did. I know why she did it, but it doesn't make it right. She wronged her own son.

He had hundreds, if not thousands, of regrets.

She'll let me out one day. And I will have my vengeance.

3

THE SCROLL DISINTEGRATED into burning embers and blew away from Zanna's fingers. "It is done," she said.

Streak gave her a serious look and replied, "And so is your time with us. You need to go."

Her mouth opened, but she swallowed her objection. Grey Cloak's stony skin started to soften, and she said, "Please, tell them I'm sorry. But I—"

"Did what you had to do? I wouldn't want to be around to tell them that. I doubt it would go well."

She edged closer to the blood brothers.

Streak blocked her with his tail. "You gave your word."

With a nod, Zanna removed her bandolier of potions, set it at Streak's feet, turned her back, and walked away. The mountain shadows cast by the tall white pines swallowed her, and she was gone.

Grey Cloak's skin prickled.

What was that?

After countless days feeling nothing whatsoever, Grey Cloak felt something, like being immersed in the water of a warm bath.

I can feel. I can feel!

Wind whistled in his ears like a shrieking siren. All of a sudden, the warmth was gone, and icy air cut him to the bone.

The pitch black began to illuminate, softly and distant at first then quickly brightening like the sun.

Light! Yes, I can see it! I'm coming!

His mind crawled toward the brightness. If his body responded, he couldn't tell. Thousands of needles jabbed him all over.

I'm either living or dying. It's better than nothing.

The shell of blackness surrounding him started to crack and give way like an egg. Icy wind kissed his face. Grey Cloak fell and hit the ground hard. He felt every bit of it.

"Ha-ha! I'm out!"

He rubbed the grit from his eyes and spit dirt. The images around him were fuzzy, and the noises were garbled.

"I can't understand you," he said. His tongue was thick, and his words were slurred. He stretched his arms and touched something that felt like the warm stones from a fireplace hearth. His sensitive fingers moved over bumpy, hard ridges surrounded by smooth, snakelike scales. "Streak, tell me that's you!"

The snout jerked up and down.

"Streak! It *is* you!" He shivered. "Oh, that's cold. Warmth, please!"

Streak's breath warmed him like toast.

"Ahh!" Grey Cloak's vision started to clear, and Streak's face sharpened. The dragon's head was twice the size of a horse's. "Zooks, how long have I been in the rock cocoon?"

"Do you really want to know?" Streak asked.

"I don't care if it's been one hundred years." He stretched out his arms. "I'm elated to be free! It hasn't been one hundred years, has it?"

Streak used his tail to place the Cloak of Legends over Grey Cloak's shoulders. "More like ten."

Grey Cloak combed his hair back with his fingers. "It felt like a thousand." He jumped. The burning wood popping sounded like thunderclaps to newly awakened ears. "Flaming Fences! Those logs sound like they're exploding."

"Master Streak, the big one is not waking up," someone said.

Grey Cloak turned around on his hands and knees. A pair of large men were lowering Dyphestive to the ground.

"He's as heavy in flesh as in stone," one of the brute men said.

"Get away from him!" Grey Cloak stumbled over to his brother.

Dyphestive's eyes were closed, and he wasn't moving.

Grey Cloak placed his ear on Dyphestive's chest. "I don't hear anything. What's wrong?" He turned back to Streak. "And where is Zanna?"

"She's gone," Streak said with a guilty expression.

Incredulous, Grey Cloak asked, "What do you mean?"

"I sent her away after she removed the spell. I thought... well..." Streak flexed his wings. "You might kill her."

Grey Cloak raised his eyebrows. "I can't say I disagree with your line of reasoning. I'd be lying if I said I hadn't vowed it over a thousand times." He caught the two rugged brutes peering over his shoulder. "And who are they?"

"Chinns and Chubb, friends of mine," Streak replied.

Grey Cloak started slapping Dyphestive's face. "Wake up, brother! Please wake up. If I can survive this, I know you can. If he dies, I'll hunt Zanna down." He bit his tongue. He'd spent what felt like an eternity plotting vengeance, but the sweet taste of life washed away his bitterness. He put his ear to his brother's chest again. "I don't hear a thing."

"Is he warm?" Streak asked.

Grey Cloak grabbed one of Dyphestive's big mitts. The

skin on his leathery palm was as cool as a cucumber. "I can't tell. I'm going to try something."

Streak came closer and gazed down at Dyphestive. "He doesn't look good. Whatever you're going to try, you'd better do it fast."

Rubbing his hands together, Grey Cloak tried to summon his wizardry, but the long-dormant magic within him did not awaken. He squeezed his eyes shut and concentrated. "Come on, wizard fire. I call on you now!" Reaching deep, he tried to stoke the mystical flames that burned within. But the coals inside his belly were cold. He strained and grunted.

"What's he doing, Master?" Chinns asked. "He sounds like he's struggling with a bowel movement."

Streak shushed him. "Is there anything I can do?"

"I hate to ask, but you need to find Zanna. You need to find her now. Only she can undo what she did," Grey Cloak replied. "I see no other way."

"Are you certain? I might not be able to find her in time."

"We don't have a choice. Find her, Streak. Find her now, before he's too far gone."

Streak nodded. "I'll be back as fast as I can. I promise." He sniffed the air, turned his head toward the front of the camp, and said, "I smell her. I hope she's not too far." He took off.

Grey Cloak hated to bring Zanna back. He understood

what Streak did and didn't fault his dragon one bit. Sending Zanna away had been the right thing. She'd done the wrong thing for the right reason. There was no telling how Grey Cloak or Dyphestive would have reacted. But they needed her. He had no idea how to save Dyphestive.

He brushed his brother's hair out of his face. "Hang on, Dyphestive. Help is coming. Don't die." Turning back to the other pair of brothers, he said, "Help me keep him warm, fellas."

4

THE FOOTPRINTS on the icy hills vanished, and Zanna's scent had been taken away with the wind. Streak could find no sign of her anywhere.

He stuck his tongue out of his mouth, caught a few snowflakes, and rolled it back in. "You couldn't have gone that far that fast," he muttered, moving his neck from side to side. "Where are you, Zanna?"

He'd sent her away, certain he'd done the right thing. She'd willingly departed, but the decision had come back to haunt him. Grey Cloak was alive and well, but Dyphestive appeared to be on the other side of dead. Something was wrong.

"Come on, Zanna!" he called. "We need your help!"

He scanned the pines bowing in the wind, fully expecting her to emerge from the shadows and say, "I told you so." He waited the longest time, but it didn't happen. He wandered farther down the hill, pushing through banks of snow and plowing over saplings and small trees. In his panic, he left a trail a blind man could follow.

He called again, "Zanna! Zanna! Where are you?"

Grey Cloak's mother had been a cauldron of mystery since her arrival. She'd worked with a dark intensity that Streak couldn't put his claw on. He liked her, but when she'd frozen the blood brothers into stone, his fondness for her had lessened.

"Listen, Zanna, now isn't the time for games. Dyphestive isn't waking up. You put him in that condition, and you need to fix him." The wind whistled by his air holes. The snowfall had started to thicken. "I know you're out there! Help them!"

He powered through the hills, over the ridges, and through the chasms and crevices. He searched inside the mouths of every cave, hoping to find her seeking shelter.

"After all these years, it comes to this." He let out an angry roar. "And now she abandons us again! I should have known. You can't trust her!"

Streak spread his wings, took a running start, and launched himself off the mountain. Then he dove downward, toward the base, and swooped across the valley. The storm in the hills was thicker than the snowfall over the plains. In the darkness, all signs of life had gone cold. The critters had burrowed away, and there were no signs of heat from a single creature.

Streak flew across the land for the better part of a league then flew back in a zigzag search pattern.

There is no way she could have made it this far. I wonder if she's hiding. How else could she have gotten away? Tricky woman.

He gave up the search, flew back, and landed back at the camp.

Dyphestive had been moved beside the larger campfire and was covered in blankets.

"You didn't find her, did you?" Grey Cloak asked with a concerned expression.

Streak shook his head. "Sorry, boss. I don't know what happened. She vanished."

"Don't trouble yourself, Streak. This isn't something we could have foreseen. I have a feeling my stubborn brother doesn't want to wake up."

"What are we going to do? I could fly to Littleton and try to find a healer."

Grey Cloak shook his head. "Desperate times call for desperate measures. I need the Rod of Weapons."

Streak went to the last spot he'd seen it and dug it out from the snow. Then he picked it up in his mouth and brought it over to the campfire.

Grey Cloak took it and said, "Thank you, brother."

"Now what are you going to do?" Streak asked.

"Wake him up with it."

Grey Cloak ran his fingers over the runes of the polished wood. The Rod of Weapons had power, but he was able to focus his wizardry into it with greater effect. He tried to summon his powers, but they were muted from his long sleep. He needed something to ignite the energy within.

He stood over Dyphestive and rested the butt of the rod on his brother's chest. "Here goes."

"Isn't it dangerous?" Streak asked.

"I'll take my chances." Grey Cloak ignited the Rod of Weapons, and blue energy shot up and flickered in his face.

Chinns and Chubb gasped and moved away.

Grey Cloak gulped. The energy in the wooden rod spread into his fingertips, through his arms, and into his shoulder. He controlled the weapon and made the spear head larger then smaller, to a narrow, burning blue tip. Then Grey Cloak flipped the rod over and held the fire over Dyphestive's chest.

"Forgive me, brother." Grey Cloak stuck the tip into his brother's heart, searing a hole in the fabric covering him.

Dyphestive didn't budge.

"Wake up, you stubborn ox," Grey Cloak growled. He fed more energy into the tip. "Wake up now!"

Dyphestive's eyelids snapped open, and his mouth

widened in a loud gasp. He grabbed the Rod of Weapons and flung Grey Cloak away as if he were a doll.

Grey Cloak sailed across the camp and into the wall of the log cabin. He slid down and landed on the porch, on his back. When he crawled back to his feet, he wasn't alone.

A hulking, wild-eyed man stood in the midst of the camp, facing the fire and clenching his fists. His jaws slavered as he stared down at Grey Cloak.

"Welcome back, brother," Grey Cloak said. "I hope that didn't hurt you too badly, but I had to do what I had to do."

Brow knitted, Dyphestive ripped off his coverings and charged.

5

"OH NO," Grey Cloak muttered.

Dyphestive descended on Grey Cloak like a bull. Grey Cloak's feet slipped on the porch as he scrambled to get out of the way.

Dyphestive hit him full force, blasting him through the cabin door and splintering the wood. They rolled across the floor, crashed through a small table, and bumped against the hearth.

"It's me, Dyphestive. Grey Cloak! Stop this!" he shouted. He ducked under a punch and tried to squirm away.

Dyphestive grabbed him by the cloak, pulled him back, and started to stuff him into the fireplace.

"What are you trying to do? Cook me?" he shouted.

His brother's eyes were glazed over.

Grey Cloak snorted with rage. "Stop it!"

Chinns and Chubb entered the cabin then hooked Dyphestive by the arms and pulled him back.

"Settle down, mate. We're all on the same side," Chubb said, straining to get the words out. "How about we go have a sit-down?"

Dyphestive roared.

Grey Cloak squeezed out of the fireplace. "Be careful. He's stronger than he looks."

"You can say that again," Chinns said. "But we can handle—"

Veins rose in Dyphestive's neck. He heaved against the brutes, flexing his arms and drawing them forward. He headbutted Chinns, breaking his nose.

"I'm not letting go, big fella!" Chinns said. "Hold him, brother. He'll wear down!"

"I don't know about that," Chubb said, his face turning red. "His muscles are still as hard as stone. I can't hold him."

Dyphestive broke free of their strong grips and pushed Chubb into the wall.

Chinns hit Dyphestive in the belly, making him double over, and put him in a headlock. "I have him! I have—*ulp!*"

Dyphestive hooked Chinns by the waist, lifted him off of his feet, and slammed him backward. *Wham!* The entire cabin shook.

Chubb tackled Dyphestive and rammed him into the wall. Dyphestive picked him up as if he were a bundle of straw and tossed him out the front door.

"Stop fighting him," Grey Cloak ordered. "Stay away from him. He needs to simmer down."

Chinns's blood was already running hot. He didn't hear a single word Grey Cloak said and bull-rushed Dyphestive. They collided in the center of the small cabin, their fists hammering away. A tooth went flying into the fireplace.

Anvils. I need to stop this before someone dies.

Grey Cloak spotted the Rod of Weapons on the floor and picked it up then turned the flame on. "Goy!"

Dyphestive knocked Chinns aside and faced Grey Cloak. His eyes locked on the blue spear tip.

"Chinns, listen to me. Go away. I'll handle this."

Gasping and sitting on his knees, Chinns said, "I ain't no quitter."

"No, but if you don't, you'll be dead."

Dyphestive's chest and shoulders heaved. He advanced on Grey Cloak, scowling.

"I always knew you had a lot of anger stored up. Perhaps now is the right time to let it all out," Grey Cloak said.

No recognition dawned in Dyphestive's eyes, only burning derangement.

"Come on, now, Dyphestive. It's me, your brother, Grey

Cloak. Dindae. You know me." He held out his hand. "Let's talk about this."

"He ain't listening, Master Grey Cloak," Chinns said.

"Get out of here, Chinns. I'll lead him out. He'll cool off."

Chinns backed through the doorway.

Grey Cloak butted against the wall and started to slide toward the door.

Get him out into the open. Anvils! I hope he isn't permanently damaged. I've never seen him this way.

Dyphestive had a history of losing himself. The Doom Riders had taken his mind and twisted it into Iron Bones, a cold, callous killing machine. Those wounds on the mind were deep. Maybe they'd reawakened.

Grey Cloak quickly backpedaled out the door, leading Dyphestive into the center of the camp.

Dyphestive's simmering eyes swept over the men and dragon surrounding him. He murmured angrily.

"He raves like a wolf," Chubb said, carrying a club. "Do we put him down, Master Streak?"

"No, of course not. Everyone has friends who have a bad day," Streak replied. "What do you think, boss? Perhaps he needs a cold bath."

"I like the way you think, but I don't see a tub of water nearby." Grey Cloak kept his eyes fixed on Dyphestive, who appeared ready to pounce at any moment. "He's about to rampage again."

"I'm prepared," Streak said.

Dyphestive rushed across the camp, bearing down on Grey Cloak.

Streak lashed out with his twin tails, coiled them around Dyphestive's ankles, and jerked him so that he fell facedown in the snow. "Get on!" he said.

Grey Cloak hopped onto his dragon's back.

Streak dragged Dyphestive through the snow and jumped off the ledge of the cliff, pulling Dyphestive along like a banner streaming in the wind. "Boy, he really is heavy."

With the chill winds rustling his hair and robes, Grey Cloak watched his brother flailing his arms and fighting to kick free. "Let me guess. You're taking him to the Great River?"

"It's the perfect spot for a hot head to cool off."

Grey Cloak nodded. "I hope it works."

When they arrived at the Great River, Streak asked, "You don't think he'll drown, do you?"

Grey Cloak leaned over the side and looked at the choppy river. "No. Drop him in."

"You're the boss." Streak let Dyphestive loose.

Dyphestive plummeted like a great stone, bellowing the entire way.

Splash! The icy water swallowed him.

Streak circled above the water. Bubbles rose to the surface then died.

"Eh, how long do you think your brother can hold his breath?" Streak asked.

"I don't know, but I guess we're about to find out."

6

"There he is!" Grey Cloak pointed. "Get down there!"

Dyphestive's head and shoulders popped out of the water downriver. He lumbered toward the riverbank with water sliding from his body and climbed onto the bank.

Streak landed several yards away from Dyphestive, and Grey Cloak hopped off and waited.

Dyphestive lifted his head and met his gaze. His burning stare had cooled.

Grey Cloak set aside the Rod of Weapons and approached slowly. "Dyphestive?"

Dyphestive rubbed his hand over his heart and asked, "Why does my chest feel like it has a hole in it?"

"Long story," Grey Cloak replied amiably. "But how are you feeling otherwise?"

"Like a dark cloud has been lifted from my eyes." Dyphestive's gaze swept over his surroundings. "How long has it been?"

"Since what?"

"You know. Since Zanna turned us into rocks."

"Oh, so you remember."

"Yeah, I remember. I remember everything." He glanced at the dragon. "Hello, Streak." He cracked a smile. "You're bigger than me now, aren't you?"

Streak went over, opened his wings, and shielded them from the wind. His chest scales started to burn like coals. "Bigger and better. Ha-ha. It's good to hear your voice again."

Dyphestive dug a finger in his ear and rolled his jaw. "Why do I feel like I've been in a fight? And why'd I wake up in a river?"

Grey Cloak took the liberty of explaining the last few events.

Dyphestive rubbed his head. "I don't remember any of that, but I'm happy to be out of the black. I couldn't stop thinking. It felt like being sealed in a coffin."

"Don't remind me."

"When we see Zanna again, I'm going to have some words for her. They won't be pleasant."

Grey Cloak helped his brother up. "Come on. Let's get back to the cabin. I could use something to eat. How about you?"

Dyphestive shrugged. "I don't even remember what

food tastes like." His belly grumbled. "But I think I need to finish that last supper we were having before Zanna interrupted it."

Chubb and Chinns prepared bowls of hot stew and brought them into the cabin, where Grey Cloak and Dyphestive were seated by the fire.

Dyphestive took his bowl, nodded, and said, "Thank you."

"You're welcome, Master Dyphestive," they said, bowing, and walked away.

"Why do they keep calling me Master?" Dyphestive asked.

Streak was lying outside. He stuck his head in the door and replied, "It's a little measure of respect I taught them while you were out. I shared a lot of stories about the both of you with them. They gobbled it up as if they were children."

"I see." Dyphestive stared into the fire. "I wondered if I would ever see light again. I don't ever want to be trapped in darkness again. All I could think about was getting out."

A chill ran down Grey Cloak's spine. "Try not to talk about it. I don't want to think about it either."

"Yeah, not thinking about it might take some time." Dyphestive ate a mouthful of stew, wiped his chin, and said, "One thing I thought about was my father. He's been trapped in stone all this time. We need to free him."

"That time is coming. We're back where we started, before we left through the Time Mural."

"Seventeen or eighteen seasons, huh?" Dyphestive took another bite. "What do we do now?"

Grey Cloak shrugged. "You know me. I'll think of something. In the meantime, let's enjoy the most delicious stew we've had in a decade."

His brother nodded. "Indeed."

They enjoyed a quiet meal together, but Grey Cloak's mind started racing. There was no certain way to know where they were in time.

He broke the silence. "I can only venture to guess that Zanna didn't bring us back until we'd overlapped the point where we originally left. That would leave Talon back at the Wizard Watch west of the Great River. We might be able to reunite with them somewhere near there."

"I'm ready when you are." Dyphestive eyed the Iron Sword, which was propped up in the corner of the room. "We both are."

"So what's the plan? Are we flying out of here first thing in the morning?" Streak asked.

Grey Cloak set down his bowl. "It's time to pick up where we left off. Hopefully, we're wiser than when we started. And let's not forget Black Frost is still in control. He'll be looking. We'll have to lie low."

Streak nodded. "What about my students?"

Grey Cloak chuckled. "Well, Master Streak, I'm sure they'll follow you wherever you want to go. After all, they were dumb enough to stay with you on the mountain for the better part of... how long?"

"Five years or so. If you don't mind, I'd like to have a word with them."

"Of course."

Chinns and Chubb were huddled by the campfire with blankets drawn over their shoulders. They stood when Streak approached.

"The time has come to depart. Hasn't it, Master Streak?" Chubb wiped his nose.

"Aye, it is."

Chinns nodded. "We knew this day would come, but we wish to come with you. We want to help."

"No, you have all the treasure you need. Use it, find wives, and start a family. Protect them and your friends. Enjoy the best of life, while you can," Streak replied.

"Master Streak, we can't enjoy life, knowing our freedom will be taken. We wish to live a legacy that frees all men from the darkness." Chubb stood shoulder to shoulder with his brother. "There is no greater treasure than freedom. That's what you taught us. We wish to fight for that."

"You aren't making this easy. You're both still as hard-headed and stupid as ever, but that's what I love about you guys. Bring it in!" He hugged them with his wings. "Stick around the mountain as long as you want. When the time comes, I'll send somebody."

7

THE SHELF

ON A CLOUDY NIGHT with rain falling softly, Streak flew across the plains. Grey Cloak and Dyphestive rode on his back. He flew little more than a few hundred feet above the land, like a giant bat in the sky.

The green plains and sweeping grasslands turned to rocky ridges, dusty ground, and clay-packed earth. They flew over the mountain peaks that divided the southern lands from the Shelf, a barren wasteland of canyons and sunken valley.

"Stay along the ridgeline, Streak," Grey Cloak said, lifting his voice above the wind. "It will be difficult to spot where we need to enter."

"We'll find it," Streak assured him. "I mean, it really hasn't been so long that we'd forget."

"Your memory is better than mine, I hope." He turned

around to Dyphestive, who was solemn and quiet. "How are you doing?"

"I'm well but looking forward to getting my feet on the ground again. It's been a long flight."

"Agreed."

They'd flown through the day and the night without their toes touching the ground once. For the majority of the journey, they'd soared through the cover of the clouds, and oftentimes, the weather had been stormy. But the last thing they needed was to cross the paths of any Riskers, and they went to great lengths to avoid them.

"It sure is black down there," Dyphestive commented.

The Shelf's terrain might as well have been an abyss. Instead of sprawling forests with blossoming treetops, only leagues of barren plains accompanied deep gorges and canyons.

Grey Cloak understood his brother's discomfort. Below them was a sea of black waiting to swallow them whole. It made butterflies flutter in his stomach. "You aren't going to be scared of the dark, are you?"

Dyphestive shrugged.

"Great." He patted Streak on the neck. "We've flown long enough. Take us down, and we'll make camp."

"You're the boss. Besides, the break will do me some good. My wings are getting a little tired." Streak glided toward the surface then pulled up and made a soft landing. "Welcome to the Shelf. Don't forget to check your baggage on the way out, and thank you for flying Air Streak."

Grey Cloak jumped off and asked, "Where do you come up with this silly talk?"

Streak shrugged. "It's called improvisation. And I dream a lot. Would you like a fire?"

"Definitely," Dyphestive said as he climbed down to the ground. "The brighter, the better."

"Not brighter," Grey Cloak said to Streak. He removed his cloak and offered it to Dyphestive. "Here, put this on."

"No, thanks. I'll manage. I'll get used to living again one way or another."

Streak scraped some brush and thorny bushes into a pile. A fiery spitball set it aflame. "Enjoy."

Grey Cloak took a seat in front of the fire, and his brother joined him.

Rubbing his hands together, Grey Cloak said, "I don't think we're far from the entrance to Safe Haven. We can walk from here, if you wish."

"That doesn't sound like a bad idea. I'd like to get my feet on the ground and get my bearings, if you know what I mean."

"Certainly." Grey Cloak looked over his shoulder at Streak, who was lying behind them.

The dragon shrugged, and Grey Cloak shrugged back.

Dyphestive's face was a mask of concentration as he

stared into the flames. He didn't bat an eyelash but was clearly out of sorts.

"Brother, you're not yourself, are you? Perhaps we should talk about it."

"I don't want to close my eyes. I don't want to sleep. I fear the darkness will take me."

Grey Cloak's heart sank. The paralyzing fear that seized his brother's mind could just as easily seize his own thoughts. Yet aside from being unable to use his powers, Grey Cloak had recovered and felt like his old self, for the most part.

But what if I have a relapse?

"Dyphestive, we can't afford to lose you to fear of the darkness," he said quietly but sternly. "Darkness is what we battle. It threatens to consume the entire world. We need you to be the rock you've always been. The time has come. You don't have a choice."

Jaw clenching, Dyphestive said, "I know, and thank you. I will give it my all. I'll do anything to help my friends."

"Speaking of which, we need to find them first. That's why I thought it best to come to Safe Haven. If they're anywhere, it would be there. Perhaps we'll have a joyful reunion."

"I wonder if Zanna knew where they were," Dyphestive said.

Grey Cloak turned to Streak.

"She didn't mention anything to me. You know how she

is—very secretive," he answered. "I know I should have beat more information out of her."

"It probably wouldn't have done any good. No, we'll find them." Grey Cloak held his hand out and caught the rain. The brush fire started dying. "Well, if no one is going to rest, we might as well start walking."

Streak stood and stretched like a cat. "Fine by me. I'm good so long as I rest my wings."

Dyphestive stood and said, "After you."

They put out the fire then walked along the base of the mountains until the new dawn began. The Shelf was a barren wasteland that stretched as far as the eye could see. On the distant horizon to the west were the great cliffs that made up the Shelf. There, the secret entrances to Safe Haven waited.

Not so long ago, the blood brothers had trained as Sky Riders over the bleak plains. They'd ridden the sons and daughters of Cinder, and Grey Cloak had battled Anya for leadership of Talon. It seemed like a day ago, but Grey Cloak felt he'd aged a score of years since. So much had changed, including him.

"Isn't this the place?" Streak asked as they came into a small valley surrounded by pinnacles shaped like jagged teeth.

"There's no mistaking it," Grey Cloak agreed. He faced the mountains, where there used to be a cave entrance to Safe Haven. It was buried in tons of rock and earth that had slid over it. "But it appears our avenue to safety is gone."

Dyphestive climbed up on the rocks and dirt that covered the entrance. He was small by comparison. He picked up a rock as big as his shoulders and heaved it down the side. "It will take some digging, but we can do it. Give me a few weeks."

"You'd love that, wouldn't you? Streak, give it a try."

"Sure." Streak started clawing at the pile like a dog. He shoveled dirt all over Grey Cloak.

"Watch out, will you?" Grey Cloak dusted himself off and moved away. "How long do you think it will take to make a hole?"

"I only just started, but I'd say it's going to take a long time, and who knows how deep it is." Streak kept scooping out dirt. "Honestly, it might be wiser to enter through Lake Flugen. It would be quicker too."

Grey Cloak kicked a clump of dirt. "Keep digging. You might have a breakthrough sooner than you think. We'll go look around and see if we can find another entrance. There are caves all over this place."

"I'd rather stay outside," Dyphestive said.

"Have it your way, but you can't hide in the daylight forever. Night will still come, brother. There is no avoiding it." He wandered away. Grey Cloak had compassion and could relate, but to see Dyphestive scared of the dark, of all things, jolted him.

The Shelf's many huge caves had openings over one hundred feet tall. Legends told of entire armies entering those massive caverns and never returning again.

Grey Cloak started up a muddy mountain on the opposite side of the dirt slide where Streak had been digging. He moved at a brisk pace, distancing himself from the others. Then he stood on a ledge and looked down.

Streak was still digging. Dyphestive picked up hunks of rock and dirt and tossed them aside. Grey Cloak smirked. From that distance, they looked like a boy and his giant hound digging in the ground together.

I think they're both enjoying this. And why wouldn't they enjoy playing in the dirt like urchins?

The ground suddenly broke away under his feet, and he slipped onto his backside. His hands sank into the mud.

Now look who else is playing in the dirt.

He climbed up and started shaking off his cloak, but the ground shifted underneath him again, and he lost his footing.

What is happening this time? An avalanche?

Two giant paws burst out of the ground, seized his legs, and yanked him hard into the muck.

8

DYPHESTIVE CLIMBED UP THE HILL, grabbed a boulder the size of a pumpkin, and hurled it to the bottom. His boots sank into the mud the more he dug, and the more he dug, the more futile the effort to find the entrance became.

On the other hand, Streak had dug half of his body into a hole when the slide started to cave in and collapse, covering the hole again. He pulled his scaly frame out, shook off the dirt, and said, "I had a feeling that was going to happen. The more I dig, the more it slides."

Dyphestive nodded. "Do you want to keep trying?"

"I'll keep going until Grey Cloak tells me to stop."

Grey Cloak had made his way toward the top of the slide and was well out of earshot.

"Maybe it's not as deep as it looks." Dyphestive grabbed a dirt clot and slung it away. "We might get lucky."

"That's a good way to look at it." Streak resumed his digging.

Dyphestive sat and watched the rain clouds pass by. As big as he was, he was no match for a mountain of dirt. "I might as well be an ant on a giant dung pile."

Steak popped his head up. "What was that?"

"Oh, nothing."

"Ah. I can tell you're out of sorts. Do you want to talk about it?"

"I don't think talking is going to do any good. I can't stop thinking about being turned to stone and the prison it became." He rubbed his dirty hands together. "I don't ever want that to happen again."

"It seems unlikely, unless Zanna shows up. And I think she learned her lesson. Don't be so down on yourself. You'll get through it. You always do."

"Thanks, Streak, but I don't want to let anyone down. I don't even want to go into a cave." He turned his face up to the gentle rain. "The darkness scares me."

"It scares us all, but we can't sulk about it. We have to move forward." Streak clawed his way back into the dirt. "I burrowed inside a cave for years, watching over the two of you, nestled in the dark and cold. It wasn't pleasant, but I'm a dragon, so it wasn't uncomfortable either. Think about it that way. You were hibernating."

"I'll try."

"Help!" Grey Cloak cried.

Dyphestive spun around. His brother was on top of the hill, being pulled down into the ground. He soon disappeared.

"I'm coming!" Dyphestive stood and started running toward the top, but his feet slipped in the mud.

In the wink of an eye, claws fastened around Grey Cloak's legs and pulled him into the cavity. He hit something hard with his fist, hurting his fingers. The big creature rolled over him, suffocating him in the dirt and using its superior weight to crush him.

I can't breathe!

Grey Cloak searched for the Rod of Weapons with his fingers, but it was nowhere to be found. He grabbed a dagger from his belt and stabbed the monster. The hard, scaly flesh of the beast didn't tear.

No. I won't succumb to the darkness again.

His gripping fear turned to anger, and wizardry ignited inside him. Energy burst out of his body.

The monster yelped and jumped off of him.

Grey Cloak scrambled out of the cavity and came face-to-face with a muddy middling dragon. He leaned toward the Rod of Weapon, which lay nearby.

Smoke steamed out of the dragon's nostrils, and his chest scales started to glow.

"Slick?" Grey Cloak asked.

The dragon tilted his head. "Grey Cloak?"

Dyphestive and Streak came rushing up the slippery hill.

"Slick!" Streak bellowed.

Slick let out an excited roar. "Brother Streak, I never thought I'd see you again!"

They bumped horns with a *clack*.

"You've gotten big, haven't you?" Slick observed.

"I've grown more over the last bushel of seasons," Streak said gleefully. "What are you doing out here?"

"Guarding the back entrance to Safe Haven." Slick shook the dirt from his body. He was one of Streak's twelve brothers and sisters and a middling dragon son of Cinder. His scales were mostly black and had a silver tortoiseshell pattern, and he had a playful yet sneaky personality. "We buried the entrance years ago, but Fenora insists that we guard it. The Riskers have been looking for it, and they scout the Shelf and search the caves. As you can see, I got the dung duty this time. Fenora is so bossy."

"It's great to see you," Streak said.

"The same to all of you. You are a sight for sore eyes." Slick shivered and turned to Grey Cloak. "What did you do to me?"

Wisps of energy danced on Grey Cloak's fingers. His wizard fire had returned. "I stopped you from suffocating me."

"Ah, I wouldn't have killed you. Just a little mud roll to knock you out." Slick gave Grey Cloak a firm slap on the back with his tail, almost knocking him over. "You'll make it." Then he draped his tail over Dyphestive's shoulders. "How have you been, big fella?"

"Well," Dyphestive replied.

Slick nodded. "Okay, then, Chatter Box. So, brothers, let's get you back into Safe Haven." He winked. "We created another safer secret entrance, and you have to know the spell to get in, which I do."

9

WIZARD WATCH

DATRIS WIPED his face with a wet towel and offered it to Gossamer.

Gossamer shook his head. They were working alone at a small forge on the top level of the tower. A cauldron of boiling metal bubbled over the flames.

Wiping his sticky hair out of his eyes, Gossamer said, "It's time to pour. Get the mold."

"Of course," Datris said. His formerly youthful face had begun to wrinkle, and dark circles had formed under his eyes. His short brown hair had grown long and shaggy, and his white cotton robes were dirty.

Gossamer was in little better shape. His black-and-white clothing was in shambles. Honzur and Commander Covis had proven to be formidable taskmasters and worked them to death. Gossamer had slept little, which wasn't unusual for elven wizards, but the work had been demanding. They had the Time Mural in full operation and were making collars that would allow them to enter the portal and be summoned back.

Datris brought over the mold for the collar. Inside the seams were small gemstones lined up in the outer circle, which matched the ones in the Pedestal of Power. He set it down beside the forge. "Gossamer, have you come to any conclusions? How will we"—he cast a quick look over his shoulder at the door—"get rid of them? It's quite an obstacle to overcome, and I can't get my head around it. I see no avenue for escape."

Gossamer moved the cauldron over the mold. "We keep buying time. Stand back." Using chains and heavy gloves, he tilted the cauldron over, and hot liquid metal poured out, filling the mold.

He had his hands full. Many seasons ago, Zanna Paydark, Grey Cloak, and Dyphestive had come to him at the Wizard Watch. Zanna told him that it was up to him to send her back in time to save the blood brothers. In order to do that, he had to master the Time Mural, replace her stone body—which resided in the bowels of Black Frost's temple—with Datris's. Disguised as Datris, she slipped back to the Wizard Watch, and Gossamer sent her back in time while escaping the dragon overlord's notice. Living out the scenario they'd described for him was difficult enough, but he'd met the challenge. But he didn't anticipate the next obstacle, dealing with the wizard Honzur and Commander Covis the Risker.

He finished pouring and watched the metal cool inside the mold. "Have faith, Datris. When the time comes, you must be ready."

"It's not easy. Are there any words you can offer that might encourage me?"

Gossamer shoved the cauldron back over the fire and managed a small smile. "An old friend of mine had a saying."

"What was it?"

"I'll think of something."

Datris's shoulders sank. "That's not very reassuring."

"No, it isn't, but it works sometimes."

Commander Covis entered the forge and asked, "Are you two pointed-eared tick lizards finished?" He strolled toward the coals, carrying a jug of wine. His long, stringy black hair hung down in front of his dark eyes, but he swept it over his shoulder and gazed into the mouth of the furnace. "Should have been me doing this. Hammering iron and steel." Three jewel-encrusted collars sat on the table, and he picked up one. "Instead, you're making jewelry. Wasted effort."

He turned to Gossamer and Datris. "If you're finished,

grab those and come on." He glowered at them. "You *are* finished, aren't you?"

"We were only letting the last one cool," Gossamer replied. "But it's ready."

Covis grabbed Gossamer by the shoulder and shoved him toward the door. "Then get going." He took a drink from his jug and looked glared at Datris. "You, too, elf. What are you waiting for? A kick in the backside?"

Datris grabbed a collar and hurried after Gossamer.

They met up with Honzur inside the Time Mural chamber. The bitter-faced wizard sat on one of the two pewter thrones that the underlings Verbard and Catten had built. He stared at the great archway, in a daze. His shell of a body was hidden inside his robes. Only his face and hands, scarred from burn marks, were showing. The many rings on his fingers twinkled in the torchlight.

Covis gave a grunt and said loudly, "Snap out of it, wizard. I've returned with the elves." He flung a collar at Honzur. "They've finished your jewelry. Now let's get this matter finished. I miss the wind in my face and the clouds beneath my feet."

The metal collar came to a stop in front of Honzur's face and hovered before his sunken eyes. He reached out and grabbed it.

"Ah, it is completed." Honzur swung his vulture-like gaze toward the elves. "How many?"

"Three are finished thus far," Gossamer answered.

Honzur arched a thin eyebrow and stood up. "Very well." He made his way over to the Pedestal of Power, stepped onto the dais, and stood behind the pedestal. A satin bag sat on the rim of the pedestal. He reached into it and withdrew a handful of sand and spread it over the precious stones inside the pedestal. Then he emptied the rest from the bag. "The sands of Bish. I think we'll start our trial there." He fastened his stare on Gossamer and Datris. "Put on the collars. We'll start this journey with the pair of you."

10

DATRIS STIFFENED. "I firmly object, Honzur. I'm one of Black Frost's most trusted servants. Certainly he would not approve of this."

"Don't get your feathers ruffled," Honzur said in a raspy voice. "You can trust me to bring you back safely."

Gossamer and Datris exchanged doubtful glances.

After clearing his throat, Gossamer said, "I understand the reasoning behind testing the trek, but using us to do that is far too risky. You'll need our assistance. We're the only others that can operate the pedestal."

Honzur scratched the ugly scar on his face and asked, "Would you rather I sent Commander Covis?"

"I'm not going through that contraption. It's wizards' work." Covis clenched his mailed fist, and the metal on his gauntlet started to glow. "Though I have wizardry in my veins, this practice is too delicate for the likes of me."

Honzur studied the pedestal as he arranged the precious stones within. "I have sought Black Frost's approval on this matter. He agrees. The two of you are the most suited for the journey."

"I don't believe you," Gossamer replied.

Covis walloped him in the belly. "Don't disrespect Black Frost's chosen one!"

Gossamer curled up on the floor, gasping for breath and clutching his stomach. Covis's punch felt like it had gone right into his spine. He coughed.

Datris knelt at his side, glared at Covis and Honzur, and said, "We aren't going anywhere without consulting Black Frost. This is madness."

"Commander Covis, will you do the honors?" Honzur asked.

Covis took the collars and snapped them around Gossamer's and Datris's necks, then he pulled both of them up by the hair. "Obey, hounds!" He shoved them toward the portal.

Gossamer wheezed. Something was wrong. Either Black Frost had sniffed him and Datris out, or Honzur had gone power mad. Either way, the mission would fail. If they entered the archway, the chances were they would never return again, and Gapoli would be doomed.

Honzur adjusted more stones and said, "Both of you

should be wise enough to believe me, but since you doubt, you give me little choice."

The gemstones in the archway pulsated, and the stone wall behind it turned into a sheet of black. Colors evolved inside the massive stone frame, and a picture began to form.

An image of a giant eye burning like a blue flame appeared. Dragon scales formed a ring around its rim.

Black Frost spoke in his monstrous voice, shaking the chamber, rustling their clothing, and rattling Covis's armor. Glaring at the elves, Black Frost asked, "Who dares disturb me?"

Honzur spoke up. "Forgive the intrusion, Glorious Master, but your servants, Datris and Gossamer, insisted on direct confirmation from you about their mission. They became very reluctant otherwise, and I wanted to be certain there were no misunderstandings."

The pupil of Black Frost's eye shifted from Honzur and settled on Datris and Gossamer. "I command that you do as Honzur states. You will explore the world of Bish, seek out Dirklen and Magnolia, and return them to me."

Datris bowed and said, "As you wish, Master, but what if we can't find them or discover they're dead?"

"I want to see what's left of them." Black Frost's burning stare settled on Honzur. "Do not disturb me again until this journey is finished." His image faded out and was replaced by a wall of stone, though his powerful voice lingered and made the floor shake. "Don't fail me. Not one of you."

With a smug look of satisfaction, Honzur said, "Now that the debate is over, we can resume your journey."

Gossamer adjusted his tight collar, which rubbed against his neck, and said, "You didn't mention anything before about finding Dirklen and Magnolia."

"Oh, I would have, but isn't it better that you heard it from Black Frost himself?" Honzur's bony fingers adjusted the stones inside the bowl of the pedestal. "Ah, I believe I have it right. Care to take a look, Gossamer? You seem to be a wizard that needs a great deal of reassurance."

"No, we are working together. I trust you."

Covis gave a deep chuckle. "Only a fool trusts a wizard."

"And what's your excuse?" Gossamer asked.

The Risker's jaw tightened for a moment, then he tossed his head back with laughter. "The black-and-white one is gutsy. I almost like it." He scratched the black hairs on his chin. "Say, how are they supposed to return with Dirklen and Magnolia with only two collars?"

"Give them yours, Commander Covis," Honzur said. "If they find the twins, they'll have to figure out that problem themselves."

Covis tossed the last collar to Datris. "I get the feeling somebody won't be coming back."

"Honzur, how are you going to know when to summon

us back? The time in one world might be different from another. We don't know."

He shrugged his narrow shoulders. "Eh, I'll give you plenty of time. We'll have to wait and see what happens. The only thing that matters to me is that we get some bodies back."

Gossamer and Datris faced the Time Mural. The stones in the archway blackened, and a whirlpool of colors formed. A land made of sand and cracked earth appeared. Dust devils and mirages formed on the horizon. Heat filled the Time Mural chamber.

Covis stepped behind Datris and Gossamer and put his metal hands on their shoulders. "It's a good thing you aren't wearing armor. It would burn you up."

"At least let us take some provisions," Datris pleaded.

Covis leaned over and spoke in both of their ears. "Nah, you're smart wizards. I'm sure you'll make do." Then he shoved them through the portal.

11

BISH: THE CITY OF BONE

"SWILL," Dirklen stated. "Pure swill!" He slung his ceramic mug, and it shattered against the wall. Purple wine dripped down to the floor.

He and his sister, Magnolia, were inside a run-down tavern in the city of Bone, in the world of Bish, which had become their home. Magnolia had laid her head on the table. Her wavy blond hair was a nest of tangles, and her dragon armor was covered in sand and grit. A bowl of cold stew rested on the table by her elbow.

The barkeep wandered over to the table, wringing a rag. He had twitchy eyes, a bald head, and a handlebar moustache. "M-My lord," he said. "Please don't destroy my property. I don't want to ask you to leave."

Dirklen chuckled. He flipped his hair over his shoulder, leaned back in his chair, and said, "Asking me to leave won't do you any good. I'm not going anywhere, apparently."

"But you're scaring away my other patrons."

Dirklen stood and towered over the man, who was two full heads shorter. Scowling, he said, "You keep this purple swill coming." He poked the man in the chest. "Do you understand me? After all, I pay."

The barkeep gulped. "Yes, but so do my other patrons. But they can't pay if they're leaving. I have many children to feed."

Dirklen grabbed the man by his shirt collar and lifted him off of the floor. Face-to-face with the frightened man, he said, "I don't care about your children. I don't care about your patrons. I don't care about anything. Do you understand me?"

"Y-Yes!"

"Good." Dirklen gently lowered the man to the floor, straightened his shirt, and patted him on his bald head. "If you will, another jug and tankard."

"As you wish." The barkeep hurried away.

Dirklen caught several wide-eyed patrons staring at him as he sat down. "What are you looking at?" he yelled.

Half of the patrons huddled over their drinks and kept their noses down, and the others headed for the exit.

Dirklen plopped into his seat. "Vermin. All of them. I've never imagined a place could be so filthy."

"Oh, will you quit complaining?" Magnolia asked. She

rolled her head from side to side, but her eyes stayed closed. "It's as foul and chronic as the weather here."

"What am I supposed to do? We've been stuck in this rathole of a world for months, trying to find a way out, and nothing."

"Yes, I know. I'm here as well. And I don't think your whining is doing us any good." She lifted her head from the table and rested her chin in her palms. "And you certainly haven't made any friends with your attitude. Lords of the Air, what is in this wine? It's foul, but I can't stop drinking it."

The barkeep returned, left a jug and a goblet on the table, and hustled away.

Dirklen gestured at the jug and asked, "Did you see that? He didn't even fill my goblet. He insults me. The daring!"

"Stop frothing at the mouth." Magnolia refilled his goblet. Her eyes were red-rimmed. "Is that better?"

Dirklen grabbed his drink and said, "You shouldn't have to do that. He's a servant." He leaned his chair back against the wall and drank. "Nasty swill."

"No one is making you drink it."

"There's nothing better to do." He rubbed the scar under his eye, which Black Frost had given him. "I will find a way out of this dirt-sucking world, find Grey Cloak, and kill him. I swear it."

"I know." Magnolia refilled her own goblet. "I've heard the news."

The twins had been stranded in Bish for months, and life had been nothing short of miserable since Grey Cloak tricked them and shoved them through the Time Mural. They'd landed in a hot bed of sand, baking underneath two hot suns.

They wandered, and a band of cutthroat brigands crossed their path. The fiendish men wanted their swords and armor, but Dirklen and Magnolia made quick work of nearly a score of men, leaving their bones and blood to feed the hot sand. They gathered the brigands' purses and left one brigand alive as a prisoner, and he led them to the City of Bone, where they killed him. They'd lived there ever since, searching for someone to help them, but help never came.

"Perhaps we should make the most of this place, dear brother," Magnolia said. "Look at these people. They could use rulers such as you and me."

"Aye, but they have their Royals to rule over them. Rulers I have yet to meet. They're a very guarded people. But let them have their dirt and sand. All I want is a wizard or a conjurer. There must be one somewhere."

She drank and said, "You know the wealthy are the most likely to have access to such people. We need to try to befriend them."

"We've tried. They treat us like dust."

"They treat *you* like dust."

"Ha, they scorn the scar on your face as well as mine. As if we're cursed."

"We *are* cursed."

The front door to the tavern opened, and a group of stalwart men strolled inside. They wore brown hats with black brims and carried long nightsticks made of polished wood. The barkeep hurried over to the men and talked quietly, subtly nodding at Dirklen and Magnolia's table.

"Well, well, well, sister, it looks like we're about to have some company."

12

A MOUNTAIN of a man with curly brown hair spilling out from beneath his hat strolled over to Dirklen and Magnolia's table. The brown-eyed man had chubby cheeks and a baby face. He wore a brown vest over a long-sleeved shirt rolled up over his meaty forearms. A gang of hard-eyed men followed him.

The big fellow pulled up a chair, turned it backward, and sat down. "I hope you don't mind."

Dirklen dropped his front chair legs down, leaned forward, and said, "Yes, as a matter of fact, I do, Constable."

The men were in the City Watch, who patrolled the streets and kept the peace. Dirklen had had a run-in with them a time or two already. "My sister and I are here minding our own business, and now, you've interrupted our meal."

"It doesn't appear I've interrupted much of anything." The large man looked over his shoulder at the wine-soaked wall and the shattered ceramic mug on the floor. "But let's not get off on the wrong foot. I'm Georgio, captain of the City Watch."

"How impressive," Dirklen said.

Magnolia nudged her brother. "Behave, Dirklen." She turned to the constable, smiling. "I want to hear what Captain Georgio has to say. After all, he's quite handsome. I'm Magnolia."

"Nice to meet you, Magnolia, And Georgio is fine, thank you." He took his hat off and set it on the table. "That's some interesting armor you're wearing. I've never seen the likes of it, and I've been around."

"Oh, did you hear that, sister? He's been around," Dirklen said.

Magnolia gave Georgio a playful look and answered, "I hope so."

"Care to tell me where you're from?" Georgio asked.

Dirklen picked up his goblet, sipped his wine, and said, "I'm positive you haven't heard of it."

"Try me."

"Listen, Captain, are you here to arrest us or make a bunch of unimpressive small talk in front of your men?" Dirklen scoffed. "It can only be one or the other."

Georgio leaned forward and said, "The two of you have been making noise in the streets for quite some time. No one knows who you are or where you came from, but they're talking. Not to mention the handful of dead bodies we discovered after you arrived. It's my business to get some clarification and make the citizens comfortable. Right now, you make them all uncomfortable. Including me."

"Oh my, a thousand apologies," Dirklen said in an exaggerated fashion. "I'm so sorry we've made so many uncomfortable in this rat's nest you call a city. My, oh my, I didn't imagine our presence would make this place any worse than it already was."

"You'd be surprised."

Dirklen stiffened, and Magnolia giggled.

"Captain, are you accusing us of something? Murder, perhaps? I'll admit to killing that goblet earlier. I'm happy to pay for its funeral and console its family."

"You're a sassy little man, aren't you?"

"Why, yes. Very deductive, Captain. Does it make you uncomfortable?"

"No, it only reminds me of someone I know." Georgio's brow knitted. "I'll ask you one more time. Where are you from? Or who are you with?"

"What are you going to do if I don't answer? Beat me with one of your little sticks?"

"No, I don't need a little stick. But I need answers. I have five dead bodies, so someone around here has blood on their hands. Could be you."

Dirklen scratched the back of his neck and said, "I don't recall killing anyone. Do you, Magnolia?"

She gave Georgio an innocent look and said, "No, can't say that I do."

"Uh-huh," Georgio replied.

"Honestly, Captain, if we killed someone, wouldn't we be hiding?"

"I've known plenty of killers that hid in plain sight."

"Well, arrest them."

"They're taken care of." Georgio put on his hat and stood back up. "I think the two of you need to come with me. No one is under arrest, but I think we need to head down to the post and get better acquainted with one another. And I'm going to need those sword belts."

"If you want them..." Dirklen stood and placed his knuckles on the table. "You're going to have to take them."

Georgio leaned on the table as well. "You really don't want to do this. Someone might get hurt."

"Oh, I plan on it."

Boots scuffled across the plank floor as the remaining patrons ran out of the tavern.

The barkeep ducked behind the bar and peeked over.

"Last warning," Georgio said.

Dirklen offered a smug smile. "I'll pass."

Georgia gave a nod, and the City Watch hemmed Dirklen and Magnolia in. They carried their black clubs in white-knuckled grips and had nervous looks in their eyes.

"Say the word, Captain," one of them said.

Georgio kept his eyes on Dirklen. "Get the lady. I'll take care of him." He moved around the table and started to crowd Dirklen then reached for his arm. "Let's go."

Dirklen hit Georgio in the jaw with a powerful, lightning-fast punch.

The captain's knees wobbled, and he fell on his backside.

"The captain! He knocked down the captain. No one has ever done that!"

"I thought he had a rock-solid jaw!" another watchman said.

"Never seen a man strike so fast," someone else added.

The astonished men lifted their clubs.

The next biggest man in the group said, "No one takes down our captain. Get them!"

As one, they attacked.

13

MAGNOLIA SNATCHED a club from a watchman's hand and knocked him in the teeth with it. A swift backhand swing broke against another man's jaw. "You're going to need more than these little sticks to harm me."

One of the men lowered his shoulder and charged like a bull. "Aaah!" He slammed her back into the wall.

She wrapped her arms around his waist, picked him up, and slammed him into a table. "You spilled my brother's wine. He won't be happy about that."

A club came down and knocked her on the head. *Crack!*

The long nightstick broke in half.

"That hurt, you buffoon!"

The City Watchman gaped. Holding his broken club, he backed away.

Magnolia seized the man by the arm, picked him up as

if he were a child, and slung him through the chairs and tables. She flipped her hair. "I receive pain, I give it."

"We can take her, men! For Bone!" one of the gutsy soldiers said. The rotund fighter was nothing but meat and muscle. He led the charge of three.

Lightning from Dirklen's fingertips blasted right through them. They shook in their boots and collapsed to the floor. Their clothing smoked.

The last one standing ran out the door.

"You shouldn't have used your powers, brother," Magnolia said. She kicked a man's arm away with her toe. "We talked about this. Now we'll be hunted."

Dirklen shook the flakes of energy from his fingers and said, "Ah, yes, but that felt so good. I needed the release."

"Brother, behind you!"

"Eh?" He started to turn.

Whop!

The watch captain, Georgio, hit Dirklen in the face so hard that Dirklen spun around, staggered across the floor, and stumbled into a table. He grabbed a chair and steadied himself.

Georgio's hair hung over his eyes. His meaty, muscular arms flexed. "You'd better not have killed any of my men."

Dirklen shook his head and rubbed his jaw. "Well, look who came back to the party. I see you want to finish your dance with me."

Georgio pointed at him and said, "I win. You surrender. Both of you."

"I don't think you know what you're going up against." Dirklen's fingers brightened and sparked. "This is going to get ugly. Are you certain you want to do this, cretin? After all, I wear armor, and you have none. You landed a good punch, but I promise you it will be your last."

"Your pretty little armor and colorful fingers don't scare me." Georgio pushed a table aside. "Let's go."

Magnolia wore a gleeful expression.

Dirklen shrugged at her. "I won't be long, sister. I'll even make it fair." He took off his sword belt and set it aside. "Now, how do you like your chances, Captain?"

"The same as before."

"Good, because you are going to lose and lose badly." Dirklen snaked toward Georgio, head bobbing. He ducked Georgio's first swing and hit the man with an uppercut to the ribs. *Crack.*

"Oh my. Did I hear something break?" Dirklen asked as he backed off. "It sounded painful. Did that sound painful to you, Magnolia?"

She'd moved behind the bar and grabbed a jug of wine. "Sounded painful to me, but don't hurt him too badly, brother. Unlike most of the rabble around here, he's cute."

Georgio hunched over, holding his ribs and wincing. "I have to admit you hit pretty hard for a little man."

"Stop calling me little. I'm as big as you, aside from a hundred pounds of fat you carry."

"What can I say? I'm a big eater." Georgio straightened his back, set his hat aside, and raised his meaty fists. "Come on. I'm awake now."

Dirklen gave him a bored look. "A glutton for punishment. Should I expect any different from a man as stupid as an ox? So be it." He lowered his shoulders and rushed toward the man. "But you really don't know what you're getting into."

Georgio started whaling away with hard and heavy punches.

Dirklen shuffled his feet, blocked, and ducked. He saw the punches coming before Georgio could deliver them, even though the watchman's skills were formidable. "I have to admit your skills are surprising. Surprisingly slow." He caught Georgio's fist in his hand. "And though you're strong, you're not nearly strong enough." In one swift move, he bent Georgio's thumb back. *Snap.*

"Aaargh!"

"Did that hurt? Good, but the pain is only beginning." Dirklen snuck under Georgio's big body and hip-tossed him across the room, into the same wall where his goblet had smashed.

Georgio slid down the wall to the floor but started to rise again.

"I see you're too stupid to know when to quit." Dirklen

crossed the room, blocked a hard punch, and rained down a flurry of his own. His lightning jabs hit the man's face half a dozen times. He had blood on his knuckles, and each punch came harder than the last. He gave the man the beating of a lifetime, cracking ribs like chicken bones.

Georgio's beefy arms absorbed some of the blows but not enough. A hard hit across his temple sent him back to the floor. He landed face-first and knocked a tooth out.

"You're making a mess," Magnolia complained. "Our little bald barkeep is going to be upset."

Dirklen studied his bloody knuckles and flexed his fingers, grimacing. "None of this would have happened if he'd let us be. Toss me a rag. The brute's head is as hard as a rock. I think I might have dislocated a finger." One of them was sticking out of place. He popped it back into the joint and wriggled it. "Ah, that's better."

Georgio stood back up. His face was swollen and bruised.

"Are you still breathing?"

Holding out his bloody tooth, Georgio replied, "Like I said. I just woke up. And you owe me a tooth."

Right before Dirklen's and Magnolia's eyes, the lacerations and bruises on the man's face started to heal.

He gave them a gap-toothed smile and asked, "How do you like me now, Dirklen?"

14

Dirklen said to his sister, "Apparently, I have underestimated the captain."

Magnolia nodded. "Looks like you might have a fight on your hands." She winked at Georgio. "I like a big, strong man."

The moment Dirklen turned back around, Georgio jumped across the floor and tackled him. He used his larger size to crush Dirklen with his body. Before Dirklen knew what had hit him, one of his arms was pinned behind his back, and his face was slammed into the floor.

He's as strong as a bull. But I'm stronger.

Neck straining, Dirklen heaved back against Georgio's strong arms. "You'll die for this."

Georgio let him go but dropped a hard elbow on him at the same time.

With the wind knocked out of him, Dirklen struggled to fight. Georgio sat on top of him and started whaling away. Dirklen's eyes started to swell, and he tasted blood. Out of the corner of his eye, he caught Magnolia standing behind the bar with a puzzled look on her face.

He flipped his hand at her. *Get over here and help me before this man punches a hole in my face!*

Magnolia squatted on top of the bar like a wild beast. She spread out her fingers, and tendrils of energy fired from the tips of her nails. The cords of white-hot light burrowed into Georgio.

Georgio's back arched, and his mouth opened wide. "Aaaugh!" His brow knitted, and with his clothing smoking, he glared at Magnolia. "You shouldn't have done that!" He clamped his hand over Dirklen's neck and started to squeeze. "But I can take all you have!"

Dirklen choked under the viselike grip of the captain. He chopped at the man's arm and, with pleading eyes, gazed at his dumbfounded sister. *I'm going to die if I don't get this man off of me.*

He reached deep inside himself and summoned his wizardry. Using the metal in his armor to channel the energy, which would otherwise burn him alive, he sent out a pulse of wizard fire.

The captain's body went flying toward the rafters and burst through one of the beams, then he came down as quickly as he'd gone up.

Dirklen rolled out of the way, and Georgio hit the ground like a stone. *Wump!*

Gasping, Dirklen crawled to a chair and pulled himself up into the seat.

"My tavern! My tavern! You're destroying it!" the barkeeper screamed.

"Stuff a boot in it, Baldy." Magnolia shoved the barkeep away and hurried to her brother's side. "Is anything broken?"

Agitated, Dirklen panted and said, "No, but look at me. I'm perspiring."

Georgio lay on the floor, groaning, and all of his clothing was smoking.

"He should be dead by now. And thanks for the help, Magnolia. What did you do? Tickle him with your fire?"

"I didn't want to destroy my hands. This sun-blasted world is bad enough for them as is."

"You could have used your sword and cut the buffoon's head off!" He started to stand. "Perhaps it's best to move on. We've drawn enough attention to ourselves."

"We?"

"Oh, come on."

Magnolia waved to Georgio, who was drooling out of the side of his mouth. "Goodbye, cute fella."

Dirklen picked up his sword belt, groaned, and started toward the exit.

Another member of the City Watch rushed into the

room. The jittery man pointed at the Riskers and said, "That's them. Right there, Officer Brak. Those are the ones who attacked the watch."

A giant of a man stooped and stepped through the doorway. With his back straightened, he stood every bit of eight feet tall. He had a nest of tawny hair. His face was tough and his features broad but not ugly. He was well-built with stocky arms and hands that could suffocate a man. The watchman wore the same clothing as the other men, only in a much larger size. His heavy gaze swept over Dirklen and Magnolia then landed on Captain Georgio and the other fallen men. "Somebody's going to pay for this."

Dirklen sighed.

"He's not as cute as the other one," Magnolia said, "but not so bad for a giant of a man. How do you want to handle this?"

"I'm tired of fooling around." Dirklen drew his longsword. The blade flickered with energy. "We need to finish this quickly."

Magnolia drew her sword as well. It glowed the same as his. "No hard feelings, Officer Brak, but we have to kill you now. Let him have it."

Energy funneled from the tips of their swords. Bolts of power coursed straight through the man, lighting up his skin and bones.

Brak's arms opened wide, and his fingers tore at the air.

He shivered all over, and an angry grimace came over his face. "Grrr!" He stepped forward, and his brooding stare turned to wildfire.

"What's happening?" Magnolia asked. "He should be dead by now!"

"I don't know, Magnolia!" Dirklen whined. "What sort of monster is this man?"

15

THE WILD-EYED OFFICER Brak hit Dirklen like a battering ram. Then he backhanded Magnolia's sword from her grip. He grabbed a handful of her wavy hair and slung her into the bar.

Dirklen lay on the floor with the side of his face kissing the wall. He turned to rise and came face-to-face with the huge man.

Brak picked him up by his armor and hoisted him over his head.

"Ack!"

The monstrous man rammed Dirklen's body into the rafters. A crack sounded.

"Thunderbolts, I hope that wasn't my back," Dirklen said. He snatched out his dagger and cut deep into the man's hand.

"Aargh!" Brak hurled Dirklen across the room toward the bar.

Magnolia ducked, and Dirklen sailed into the shelves of jugs and bottles. *Crash!*

Sour wine and rotten ale soaked him, and broken bits of ceramic and glass covered him. He started to rise but slipped. "This is getting ridiculous! Who are these people?"

"Brother, help me!" Magnolia called.

Brak lifted her above his head, getting ready to throw her.

Dirklen charged his dagger with energy and hurled it into Brak's gut.

Snarling, Brak threw Magnolia at Dirklen. He ducked, and she slammed into the wall.

She glared at her brother. "Thanks for catching me."

"What am I supposed to do?" He peeked over the bar to see that the berserk man was coming their way. "We need to be smart about this, or he'll kill us." He spotted his sword lying on the other side of the room. "We have to cut him down."

Brak reached the bar, grabbed the edge, and ripped the top off. He hit Dirklen with a hunk of wood.

Magnolia crawled out from behind the bar. "Hello?" she said to Brak.

"Rahr!" Brak stomped toward her.

Dirklen took a running jump and landed on Brak's

back, locking him in a chokehold. "Get a sword! Get it and kill him quickly!"

Magnolia kicked though broken pieces of furniture on her way to grab one of their swords.

Brak punched over his shoulders at Dirklen's head.

He moved out of the way. "You missed, buffoon!"

Brak turned his back to one of the room's support beams and smashed Dirklen into it repeatedly.

"Ulp!" Dirklen held on to the brute's neck, using every ounce of strength in him. "Magnolia!" His back smacked against the beam again. "Hurry!"

She picked up a sword, and her eyes lit up like lightning. The blade glowed with angry fire. "Time to finish this!" She gripped the sword in both hands and charged.

"Yes, sister. Yes!"

But Magnolia tripped over Captain Georgio's arm.

He came to life and dragged her to the ground. "No, you don't." He wrenched the sword from her hand. "I hate to hit a lady, but you give me no choice." He punched her jaw.

She turned her head aside, narrowed her eyes at him, and punched back.

Georgio's head rocked back. "You really can hit hard."

Magnolia hit him again. *Whop!*

He tackled her, and they wrestled across the floor in a tangle of armor, muscle, hair, and limbs.

Brak slammed Dirklen into the beam. "Get off of me!"

But Dirklen held on. "No. I'm going to kill you first!" He

cranked up the pressure on the man's bullish neck, gasping and straining.

Brak let out a wild yell and rammed Dirklen clear through the support beam. They tumbled to the floor. Dirklen's grip broke loose.

The beams above their heads started to groan. Then the entire second floor came down.

Georgio pushed his body out of the wreckage. Dust covered the place. He coughed a few times and cleared his throat.

The rooms on the second floor of the small tavern had collapsed over most of the room. Several people were sprawled out on the broken ground. A woman was still sitting on her bed, shaking like a leaf with her covers drawn up to her nose.

Brak sat up beside the woman, and she shrieked.

With a grunt, Brak shook the dust from his hair. "What happened?"

As big rats scurried across the planks and vanished into the fallen wood, Georgio went over and helped Brak up. "We had some visitors, and you went berserk," he said.

Brak studied the area. "Did I do this? Huh. It looks like my work." Burn holes in his clothing were smoking. "I feel like I've been on fire."

"You were, so to speak. Those people were wizards or

something. Never seen the likes of them." Georgio scanned the rubble. "Probably Royals. After all, they acted like arses. I think they had enough and escaped. Dirty rats."

Brak picked up a dagger from the ground. Blood was on the metal. "Was this in me?"

Georgio lifted Brak's shirt, saw the bloody gash in his stomach, and said, "You'd better get that taken care of. It looks bad."

Brak fingered the wound. "It feels like it's cauterized already. I'll manage."

He and Georgio started picking through the debris. Some of his men were still breathing, but others hadn't made it. "I swear, if the Royals did this, they'll have a war on their hands."

Brak lifted the heavy wooden post he'd broken and set it upright. "I remember seeing their faces now. A man and a woman with scars running down their cheeks. They shot me with lighting from their swords. I've seen plenty of Royals, but I've never seen them do anything like that before."

Georgio spotted a sword handle buried in the wreckage and pulled it out. The craftsmanship was marvelous. It had polished handles and a cross guard plated in a strange black and silver, and the blade shone like daylight. He thumbed the razor-sharp edge and cut himself. The small laceration quickly healed. "I've never seen craft quite like it." He grinned. "I bet it's worth a fortune."

"We should show it to Melegal. He'll know what it's worth."

"That sourpuss." Georgio frowned. "I'd rather cash in first."

16

SAFE HAVEN

THE CAVERNS of Safe Haven led to an underground land that went on for leagues. Great rock formations held glinting stones and had ceilings that gave off light like stars. Subterranean lakes filled with crystal-clear water dotted the land along with strange spongelike plants and mushrooms twice as big as men.

Slick led the way through the valley with his dragon tail twitching from side to side. The walk had been long, and Grey Cloak's legs began to tire. After spending close to a decade in stone, his body hadn't come around. Some of his limberness was gone, and his joints ached.

"How are you feeling, brother?" he asked Dyphestive, who had a glum look on his face.

"A little rigid."

"Agreed, but I'm glad it's not only me."

Slick swung his head back around and said, "Everyone is going to be so glad to see you. They're all itching for action. We'll head to the armory. Nath is always in there, staring at the Pedestal of Power. I think he's been looking for you."

"Seek, and ye shall find," Streak said. With a flap of his tail, he sliced off a hunk of yellow mushroom and ate it. "Mmm. I missed these things. It's not steak and potatoes but an adequate substitute."

"Hello," Slick called. They hadn't seen a dragon from Cinder's family yet. "Hello? Where is everyone?"

"As I recall, a lot of them like to hide," Grey Cloak said.

"That's true, at least as far as the big boys are concerned. But Fenora and Feather are always in everyone's business. There. I see them, up at the armory's entrance." Slick grinned, showing his long, sharp teeth. "Let me go ahead. I can't wait to see the looks on their faces."

Fenora rose on all fours and eyed the group coming her way. The grand had a gorgeous jade-colored pattern all over her scales. Her matching eyes locked on Slick, and she yelled, "Brother, why have you abandoned your post? And who are... Streak!" She jumped up and ran toward them. "Grey Cloak and Dyphestive! Shades of the Dragons, tell me it's you!"

"It's us!" Streak said proudly.

He and Fenora butted horns.

"Look at how you've grown," she said. "You're closing in on me!"

"I've been drinking a lot more dairy."

Fenora let out a dragon call.

From the front of the Armory, Feather came running. The middling dragon had pretty pink scales in a tortoise-shell pattern. "Oh my, oh my, oh my! I can't believe it's you! Everyone thought you were lost in the Wizard Watch."

"We were, but it's a long story," Streak said.

Before long, everyone was greeting one another and getting reacquainted.

A charge of energy flowed through Grey Cloak at the arrival of the excited dragons. Slicer and Chubby were the last middling dragons to appear. Slicer's bright-blue scales shone, and he spoke in a velvety voice, while Chubby was heavyset and dragged his belly underneath him.

Bellarose, a grand dragon splashed with lavender, appeared and greeted them with a warm voice and sleepy eyes.

Finally, the rest of the grands showed up—Rock, a big black dragon with dark eyes and muscular scales, followed by Snags and Smash, the brutes of the family. The only ones that didn't appear were the triplets, the red, blue, and white middlings who didn't say a word and always clung to Cinder's side.

"Well, I don't know about the rest of you, but I'm going

to burst if you don't tell me where you've been," Feather said. She gave Grey Cloak a nudge with her wing.

"Like Streak said, it's a long story—"

Rock stomped. "I like a good story. Out with it." He had a flat head and a bullish neck, built more like a larger Streak.

"Yeah!" the deep-voiced Crush agreed.

"All right, but can't it wait until after we meet with Nath?"

The dragons crowded them. "No!" they all said.

"So be it."

Grey Cloak started with the battle at the Wizard Watch and how Gossamer's betrayal had sent them back in time. His audience was fully captivated. He told them about the barbarians in Ice Vale, encountering Zanna Paydark, her betrayal, and how she'd turned them to stone.

"So that's where we've been the last score of seasons. But to all of you, it's only been a season, if that, since we departed."

"Is all this true, brother Streak?" Fenora asked.

"Every bit of it. I'd have a hard time believing it myself if I hadn't been there."

With a nod, Fenora said, "Nath is going to want to hear all of this. But I had to be sure your story was legitimate. Come on. He's in the armory. He's *always* in the armory."

"Lead the way," Grey Cloak said.

The armory was a huge cave big enough for a grand

dragon to enter. Weapon racks of the finest craft were lined up in rows, and suits of dragon armor were hung up all over.

Grey Cloak and Dyphestive entered the deep chamber and moved to the rear, where the Pedestal of Power chamber waited.

"We'll wait out here," Fenora said. She and Streak were the only ones that had come inside the armory. "I want to pick my brother's brain a little more. And let me warn you, Nath has been a little grumpy lately."

"Why?" Dyphestive asked.

"He won't say, but something seems bad."

17

NATH STOOD HUNCHED over in front of the Eye of the Sky Riders. His back was to Grey Cloak and Dyphestive. His long gray hair hung down to his shoulder blades, and streaks of red shone through. His scaly hands rested on the pedestal's rim.

Three dragons known only as the triplets surrounded the dais. They were lying down, like hounds by a fire, guarding their master. They were pretty middling dragons, all girls, and each had scales of a different soft powdery color—one red, one blue, and one white. None of them moved an inch, but their eyes were open and fixed on the brothers.

"Knock, knock," Grey Cloak said.

"Do my ears deceive me?" Nath turned. "Tell me my

eyes don't deceive me as well. Is that truly you, or am I seeing ghosts?"

"It's us. Flesh and blood, you crazy old hermit," Grey Cloak said.

Nath ambled down the dais, hopped over the white triplet's tail, and hugged Grey Cloak and Dyphestive at the same time. "I can't believe it! I'm elated! I felt for certain you were gone."

Trapped in Nath's bearish grip, Grey Cloak managed to say, "No, we still live and breathe." Nath was older but taller and still had a great deal of strength in his limbs. "For the moment."

Nath gave them both one last squeeze. "Gads! I'm elated." He backed off and held their cheeks in the palms of his scaly hands. "Let me get a look at both of you." His golden eyes glimmered with new life as he searched their faces. "You've been through some trials, haven't you?"

"That's one way of putting it," Dyphestive said, taking his hand and shaking it. "It's good to see you, Nath. And how've you been? Fenora mentioned you haven't been yourself."

"Ah, yes, well, I've been filled with nothing but despair of late." The skin on Nath's strong, angular face was sagging, and his wrinkles had deepened. "I can still feel my home dying, like a candle melting to a nub. I hate to say it, but little has gone right since you vanished."

"What do you mean? Where's Talon? We thought they might be here," Grey Cloak said.

Nath shook his head, a sad expression on his face. "I only wish they were. Without you, they moved on with the quest to stop Black Frost."

Grey Cloak's chest tightened. "Please tell me they aren't dead."

"No, I don't think so. I believe they're quite alive, but I'm certain they wish they were dead."

"What's going on, Nath?" Grey Cloak demanded.

"After you were lost, they returned here. Using the Pedestal of Power, Tatiana hatched another plan to stop Black Frost. She searched for the Dragon Helm and found it." Nath headed back to the Eye of the Sky Riders. "Join me."

"When you say she found it, do you mean she has it?" Dyphestive asked as they joined him by the marble pedestal.

"No, she only discovered its location. Talon went on a journey to recover it weeks ago." Nath passed his hand over the Eye of the Sky Riders. The sand inside came to life, and an image formed, showing an aerial view of a great mountain range. "These are the Peaks of Ugrad, where their search began."

Grey Cloak and Dyphestive leaned over the image.

"That's a long way," Grey Cloak said. "Who has the

Dragon Helm? Don't tell me Black Frost. Those mountains are closer to him."

"No, Tatiana found the Dragon Helm lying in a very discreet location. It's behind the Flaming Fence. They went there."

Grey Cloak almost swallowed his tongue. "What are you talking about? The Flaming Fence? That's not a real place."

"It's all too real, I'm afraid."

Dyphestive and Grey Cloak shared blank looks.

"I thought it was a story to scare children," Dyphestive stated.

"No, it's all too real but often forgotten about," Nath said. "Long ago, there was the Time of Troubles. Giants, dragons, and the races battled for world domination. All sides were split between good and evil. The righteous efforts of the good prevailed, and the wicked ones were banished into the bowels of the mountains and sealed in with the Flaming Fence."

Grey Cloak stared into the misty, snow-capped peaks. "If they go in, how are they supposed to make it back out? Won't the flames kill them?"

"The fires trap the wicked, not the good."

"That's preposterous," Dyphestive said. "They shouldn't have done that. You shouldn't have let them do that."

"I didn't send them. They did what they felt must be done. And I agree that it was the only hope to defeat Black

Frost. I can think of no other way." Nath sighed. "I'm sorry. I watch the hills day and night, but there haven't been any signs of them. And my skill is not so great as Tatiana's. She was able to get a glimpse into the location where the Dragon Helm was."

Grey Cloak wanted to pull his hair out. The thought of his friends being trapped behind the Flaming Fence was maddening. "We have to go after them. They must be suffering." He glared at Nath. "Why didn't you go after them?"

"Believe me. I've been seeking help, but this mission is beyond my abilities. We are all that we have left. With or without the Dragon Helm, we will have to find a way to defeat Black Frost, if they don't make it. I still have faith that they might escape. I'm giving them time."

"*Time?*" Grey Cloak shouted. "Sounds to me like you've wasted enough time!" He jumped off the dais and stormed away.

18

"WE'VE HAD a hard time over the last decade," Dyphestive said to Nath. "Literally."

"What do you mean?"

Dyphestive shared everything they'd gone through. He always enjoyed talking to Nath, who brought peace and calm, unlike the feisty hermit he used to be.

"I haven't been just standing here, abandoning Talon. They're my friends too. But we can't blindly rush into the unknown," Nath explained. "I fear they might have been in over their heads, but I'm not sure of a better choice."

Dyphestive looked back at the chamber's exit where Grey Cloak had fled. "He'll be back. And I'm sure we'd have tried the same thing Talon did. But we have to find a way to save them."

"We will, but it sounds to me like we need to help you

overcome your fear of darkness. You can't go into the Cavity of Chaos if you fear the dark. A place such as that will suffocate you."

"I can only hope it will pass. But I was in stone for so long that all of my thinking couldn't beat it. Nothing has ever rattled my skull like that before."

"Do you mind if I try something?"

Dyphestive shrugged. "Go ahead."

Nath touched his fingers to Dyphestive's temples and searched his eyes. "Relax. This will only take a moment."

Warmth like the dawn of a new day passed into Dyphestive's head. A spring of vitality spread through him. They stood eye to eye, looking deep into the depths of each other. Part of Nath became a part of him, and part of him, Nath.

In a hushed voice, Nath said, "You have darkness deep within you. It feeds on your fear from something long ago, not from when you turned to stone. I see evil men. A woman."

"The Doom Riders," Dyphestive muttered. "They turned me into a killer." A tear ran down his cheek. "I slew the innocent and shed their blood."

"You must learn to forgive yourself and move on. I can see what you did was wrong, but you didn't have control over yourself. You were manipulated." Nath's golden eyes brightened and drew him in. "But you have done right ever since. Trust the good in you. It's deep. Let the light in you suffocate the darkness." He stepped away.

Dyphestive's knees gave way, and Nath caught him.

He felt as light as a feather, as if a great stone had been removed from his shoulders. Regaining his footing, he wiped his eyes. "What happened?"

"There was poison in you, and I was able to kill some of it. I've experienced the likes of it before."

"Poison?"

"I think the Doom Riders did more damage to you than you realized. You might have been fed a concoction and not known it. It allowed them to control you longer. But you're a healer, and your physical wounds can heal, but the ones inside your spirit were damaged as well." Nath squeezed this shoulder. "I hope this will set you right."

"I do feel better."

Another light appeared inside the chamber.

"Dalsay," Dyphestive said.

"Yes, it is I, and I must say I didn't expect to find you here, Dyphestive. Well met."

"Indeed." He yelled out of the chamber, "Grey! Grey! Dalsay's here!"

Grey Cloak ran inside moments later and joined them. "Tell me you bear good news."

"Quite the opposite," Dalsay admitted. "I hate to inform you that our companions are held in the Nether Realm by the Speaker of the Realm, who is called Utlas. The retrieval of the Dragon Helm was a trap set up by Black Frost. I believe we've had a traitor in our midst. A changeling, perhaps."

Dyphestive and Grey Cloak exchanged stunned looks. "We dealt with a changeling in Ice Vale."

Dalsay nodded. "And Talon encountered another on their journey to the Black Foothills. It seems Black Frost has known or at least accurately anticipated our every move."

"How do you know all this? And how did you escape?" Dyphestive asked.

"I remained hidden. That was the plan." Dalsay glided over to the Eye of the Sky Riders. "I can show you, but you won't like what you see. The Nether Realm is a terrible and deceitful place. It fooled Talon, and it fooled me. But the light of truth reveals all evil."

The image inside the eye dropped from the sky to stark hills then fell rapidly through the caves.

Nath raised his gray eyebrows. "He's far more skilled with the Eye than I was."

They leaned over the image. Deep in the earth were bridges that crossed over great chasms. The last one was made from skulls and bone. There was a chamber of skulls, a great doorway, and beyond it a wall of fire stretching as far as the eye could see.

"The Flaming Fence. They're on the other side." Dalsay searched their faces.

"Take us through," Grey Cloak said.

The Eye of the Sky Riders moved through the deep wall of flames. A vast underground kingdom awaited them. The stone buildings were tall and ugly. Tens of thousands of people from all walks of life wandered the streets. Their skin was gray, and their eyes were bright like flames.

"Those are people? What happened to them?" Dyphestive asked.

"They have adapted to their harsh subterranean surroundings, aided by magic, a deep will to survive, and a yearning to escape. It keeps them going. And Black Frost has made a pact with them to release them." Dalsay passed a hand over the image. "We can't allow that to happen."

"Where are our friends?" Grey Cloak demanded.

The image moved over a huge temple-like structure with a long row of steps then moved past the highest dome of the deteriorating building and dropped down over the other side. At the back was a steep drop into the wall of flame. Rocks with huge metal cages floated high above the fire.

Zora, Tatiana, Gorva, Beak, and Razor were inside one of them. Their heads were down or pressed against the bars. They looked defeated.

Dyphestive leaned away from the picture and said, "We're going to get them." His jaw muscles clenched. "We're going now."

19

GREY CLOAK'S STOMACH SANK. The distraught expression on Zora's face had broken his heart. She was a woman defeated.

"How do we get in there?" he asked.

"That's a problem," Dalsay answered. "Tatiana used the Star of Light to shield them from the flames. You'll need an incredible energy shield to get you through. Not to mention that Utlas took the Star of Light."

"Why in the world did they go in there? It's too danger-ous," Grey Cloak said. "You have to find a way to get us in. One way or the other, we're going to save them."

"Not to sound fatalistic, but they knew what they were attempting. Utlas told them of Black Frost's trap. The people of the dead want you to try to rescue Talon, but you would be trapped as well." Dalsay moved his ghostly hand away from the picture, and the image started to fade.

"Bring it back," Dyphestive said.

"I will not. They'll sense us watching. The last thing we want to do is lead them to our location." Dalsay glided back over the dais. "There is more. Black Frost ordered Utlas to destroy the Dragon Helm. Chances are that it is gone already."

"No." Dyphestive slammed his fists on the pedestal. "We can't give up. And we will save them."

Dalsay sighed. "I can find a way in for you, I'm certain, but I fear your attempt will be futile. Perhaps if Black Frost destroys the Flaming Fence, our companions will be freed."

"Or they'll be killed." Dyphestive turned to Grey Cloak. "We have to save them now."

"I'm thinking." Grey Cloak didn't know where to start. Ugrad was a long way away, but even more difficult would be passing through the Flaming Fence and escaping with his friends while being chased by hordes of angry people. He thought of his mother, Zanna. She might be the only person who knew the way, but she was gone.

"What about Anya and Bowbreaker?" Dyphestive asked. "I didn't see them in the cage. And where did Beak come from?"

"Anya and Cinder joined the others to find help."

"What others?" Grey Cloak asked.

"Crane, Tinison, and a mountain guide named West. I imagine they've moved back into the south."

"What about Bowbreaker?" Grey Cloak asked. "He was with us when we left."

"He was elsewhere."

"Elsewhere," Grey Cloak stated. He'd never had a great fondness for Bowbreaker. "That figures."

"What about the Wizard Watch and the Time Mural, Grey? Perhaps we can use that."

"You can't," Dalsay said. "If Nath didn't inform you already, Gossamer destroyed the Wizard Watch shortly after you were sent through it."

Dyphestive started to speak but caught Grey Cloak giving him a look and closed his mouth.

"Dalsay, what do you have to do to find a way in?" Grey Cloak asked.

"I'll have to do research at one of the watchtowers. It will take some time," he answered.

"Well, what are you waiting for?"

The gaunt-looking Dalsay nodded and said, "I'll return shortly." His ghostly body vanished.

"What was that all about, Grey?" Dyphestive asked.

"How do we know he's not part of the problem? You heard him. There might be a traitor among us, and it might be him."

"He's a ghost."

"He's a wizard, and they are the reason for this entire

mess." Grey Cloak brushed his hair out of his eyes. "We have to make sure we can trust people."

With a curious expression, Nath asked, "Am I missing a vital piece of information?"

Grey Cloak said to Dyphestive, "Go ahead and tell him."

"So, Gossamer sent Zanna back in time to help us. He rebuilt the Time Mural." Dyphestive squinted an eye. "This gets a tad confusing."

Grey Cloak held a hand out. "Let me try. Gossamer has been playing Black Frost all along. He sent us back to the past to protect us. He destroyed the mural and was supposed to rebuild it again to send Zanna back to rescue us. She came back, so he must have rebuilt it. In the meantime, we contacted Gossamer in the past and told him what needed to be done. If all goes well, he'll resend Zanna back, and we can use the Time Mural again."

Nath held his chin and rubbed his cheek with a long, scaly finger. "So Gossamer has rebuilt the Time Mural?"

"It would have happened shortly after we were banished to the past," Grey Cloak said.

"That's been many weeks. But if he's rebuilt the Time Mural, we'll be able to use it again to our advantage." Nath flashed a smile. "This is great news. But we need to find someone that can tell us it's done. And we sent the perfect candidate to do that away."

Dyphestive frowned at Grey Cloak.

Grey Cloak smirked. "What? You know we haven't had the best of luck with wizards."

Dalsay reappeared. "Oh, don't worry, my friends. Your fortune is about to change. I heard everything." He smiled. "I will get this done. You have my solemn word. For Talon."

20

THE NETHER REALM

RAZOR SAT with his hands and legs sticking through the bars of the cage. His face rested against the metal, and his eyes were closed.

Zora fought the urge to weep. She was caught in a situation unlike anything she'd ever imagined—caged on a slab of rock that floated over a wall of fire. They had nowhere to go but down to their deaths.

A grand dragon with scales that looked like stone flew by, a hungry look in his burning eyes. Many had sailed through the blistering skies of the Nether Realm.

Time passed, and no one said a word. Shock had settled in quickly after Utlas served them their sentence. Eventually, blame would go around. Zora felt the burden on her shoulders.

She sniffed. No one noticed, or if they did, they didn't show it.

Tatiana sat cross-legged near the middle of the rectangular cage, her eyes closed and her hands on her knees with her fingers facing upward.

Gorva, a brute of an orcen woman, stood with her arms crossed over her chest, staring at the kingdom city on the edge of the cliffs. Her brow knitted, and sweat glistened on her skin.

Leaning against the bars in the corner was Beak, the daughter of the Monarch Knight Adanadel. Her head was buried between her knees.

Zora had never seen a more defeated group of people. They'd gotten in over their heads, and she was to blame.

Who was I to believe we could travel through the Flaming Fence and dupe an entire army? What was I thinking? I'm not even a natural.

Other rocks with cages floated by. The people inside them were worn and haggard. All hope had fled from their eyes. Their thick skin would not save them.

Razor began to whistle a cheerless tune.

Not long after, Gorva asked, "Will you stop doing that?"

He rolled his face across the bars and gave her a sideways look. "You don't like my whistling, darling?"

"Please don't call me that," Gorva said flatly.

Razor turned all the way around. "Ah, don't be like that.

Given the graveness of our predicament, perhaps it's time we revealed our situation."

Zora sat up, and Beak lifted her head.

"What situation?" Zora asked.

Gorva frowned at Razor. "Don't you dare say a word."

He grinned. "We're in a romantic relationship."

"No, we aren't," Gorva replied.

"She kissed me in an alley. Back in Farstick. It was a long, wet one." He beamed. "I have to say it was one of the best kisses I've ever had."

"If looks could kill, Razor would be a dead man now," Beak said and followed it with a chuckle. "The two of you. Oil and water. Who would have imagined." She erupted in chuckles and had to hold her gut.

"What's wrong with her?" Gorva asked with an incredulous expression. "See what you've done, Razor?"

"Well, if we're going to die, I want everyone to know that you love me." He stood. "Come here, my sweet." He approached her with open arms. "I bet Tatiana could perform our ceremony."

Gorva smacked him. "Come to your senses, man. We need to find a way out of here. Not court one another."

He rubbed his jaw. "Ow. Even the other side of my face felt that." He raised an eyebrow. "But that was an admission."

"What was?" Gorva asked.

"You said *we* were *courting* each other. You heard her. Didn't you, Zora? There's no denying it!"

Gorva rolled her eyes and turned away.

Zora wiped her damp locks from her forehead. "Well, I didn't hear a denial about that kiss."

"I didn't either," Razor replied.

Gorva turned her head over her shoulder. "I am an honest woman. Yes, I kissed him. I could not think of a better way to shut him up. I gave in to a moment of weakness."

"Ah, it was more than that," he said.

"I'm sure we all have our regrets," Zora stated.

"Regrets?" Razor tapped his chest. "I don't have any regrets. And she doesn't either. That was a moment. It was living. And moments like that are worth fighting for."

Beak's giggles subsided. She wiped her eyes and said, "Oh, I needed that gut buster. You and Gorva. Whew! That's funny."

"It's not that funny," Gorva said.

"All right, it's not funny—only startling, especially after the countless times you've brushed him aside," Zora said with a smile. "Well, it *is* funny."

"Can we stop talking about kissing? It happened. It's over. We need to move on." Gorva moved to the bars and sighed. "Don't make me jump into that fire."

"His kiss couldn't have been that bad," Beak said.

Gorva bumped her head on the bars.

"That's enough. Leave my beloved alone," Razor said. "I don't want to see her upset on our wedding day, if this is it."

Gorva turned around, grabbed Razor by the collar, and lifted him up on tiptoe. "Will you stop the foolish talk? I am not your betrothed!" She shoved him away.

Razor stumbled backward toward the cage bars. He lost his footing and passed right through them then fell over the edge of the rock.

Zora gasped, and Gorva leapt over.

"*Help!*" Razor hung on to a small lip of the rock, his entire body dangling over the Flaming Fence.

"I'm here!" Gorva slid on her belly, reached over the rim, and seized his arm. "I won't let you go." Her body started to slide across the slab of rock. "But who's got *me*?"

Zora and Beak dove for Gorva's legs and towed her backward as she hauled Razor up.

Razor scooted away from the edge, panting, his face as pale as the moon.

Thunderous laughter came from afar. The giant Utlas stood on a slab of rock that floated above them. He glowered down at them with his pitch-black eyes, waved, and said, "Careful, mortals. Your footing is not as solid as it seems."

21

BISH

DRY HEAT STIFLED GOSSAMER. His blistered feet felt like they were on fire. He'd never walked so much in his life. Not even the icy stairs reaching into the lofty heights at Black Frost's temple matched the hot, forsaken land he trod on now.

"This is a miserable place, isn't it?" Datris asked as he tipped over his boot and let sand run out. He squinted up at the burning balls of fire in the sky. "I had gotten used to the cold, but I don't like the heat."

"And I thought the cold was bad." Gossamer rubbed the sand out from between his toes. They'd been walking hours on end since they arrived on Bish, following a faint road that had to lead somewhere. "This is worse."

A scorpion scurried across the sand and buried itself.

"Ugly little creatures. There are so many," Datris said. He ran a finger under his metal collar. "This burns."

"Mine's hot too." Gossamer scanned the horizon. The land was nothing but haze all around, with mirages as far as he could see. "We'll need water soon. If we don't find it, we'll be food for the scorpions."

Honzur had given the elves an impossible task. They were in a world where they knew nothing and would be lucky to survive a few days.

Grimacing, Gossamer pulled his soft leather boot on. "The suns are starting to set. We'd better keep walking and hope we find shelter soon."

Datris stood and wiped the sand from his robes. "What do you suppose the people here are like? It's a rugged place."

"I don't know, but I hope we find out. We're going to need all the help we can get. Tatiana found some assistance, so we can only hope we can locate the place called Bone and possibly get some answers."

Tatiana had shared a good deal of information with him after her excursion to Bone. She'd met some people and told them about the underlings Verbard and Catten, piquing their interests. If he could find the same people, they might be of some help in the search for Dirklen and Magnolia.

Pressing forward against the wind, Gossamer and Datris covered their eyes. The road disappeared from time to time, only to reveal itself again. It didn't seem as if anyone had traveled down the road in a long time.

A distant rumble caught Gossamer's attention, and he turned. A cloud of dust appeared on the horizon.

Datris shielded his eyes. "What do you think it is?"

"Galloping horses. Looks like soldiers." He pushed Datris off the road.

"What are you doing? They can help us."

"We need to get a better look at what's coming first. Let's hide in the rocks."

Datris shook his head. "I think we'd better at least ask where we're going." He remained in the road. "I'm sure they'll stop."

"Don't be naïve. This is a dangerous place." Gossamer tugged Datris by the arm, but he resisted.

Cavalry thundered toward them. Soldiers in full suits of black armor rode dark stallions. A bloodred-and-gold banner waved in the front of the ranks.

Datris lifted his arms and started to wave, but the troops bore down on him and didn't slow. He paled, dropped his hands, and ran off the road.

The cavalry raced, hooves pounding the ground, creating a giant dust cloud. A score of soldiers passed by and were gone without giving Datris and Gossamer so much as a glance. They disappeared over the next rise, and the thunder went with them.

"If I hadn't moved, I'd be ground meat, wouldn't I?"

Gossamer fanned the dust and coughed, clearing his dry throat. "Yes, I don't think they'd stop for anyone, least of all us. My heart is racing, but at least we know this road leads somewhere."

A ring of a bell and the rattle and squeak of a wagon caught their ears. Both of them turned.

A mule pulling a cart came toward them through the dust. The driver sat on a bench seat built for one. The cart moved at a quick pace and slowed down the moment the driver saw Datris and Gossamer.

"Whoa, Quickster. Whoa!" a halfling called in a child-like voice, though he wasn't young. He carried a fan and started waving the dust away. "Bloody Royals. About ran me over, they did. Think they own everything." He looked Gossamer and Datris over. "Looks like they almost got the best of you too." He smiled. "You walking to Bone? Still have a long way to go. And I don't think those shoes will hold up. The ground will burn your feet, unless you're a fleet-footed halfling like me." He stuck out his foot, which was as big as a regular-sized man's, if not bigger. "My feet can handle anything."

"Pardon, sir, but we could use a lift. We are... well, adrift, so to speak," Gossamer said.

Datris licked his cracked lips, eyed the water jugs hanging from the wagon, and said, "And a drink would be so kind."

The halfling leaned forward, squinted, and gave them

both a once-over. "You have strange ears. Need to cover those up, or the Royals will snatch you up. Anything different, they'll claim it." He tugged at his goatee. "I don't know. What do you think, Quickster?"

"You call your mule Quickster?" Gossamer asked.

"No, don't ever say that. He'll be offended. He's a quick pony, he is. Not a mule or a donkey. If his master heard you say that, he'd gore you."

Quickster was loaded down with packs of gear. The fuzzy-bellied mule shook his ears and snorted.

The halfling slapped his hands together and said, "He approves. Climb in if you like and grab a drink. But don't rummage through my treasure. Understand?"

Gossamer and Datris nodded. "Thank you," they said as they climbed in.

"Don't mention it. Oh, and my name's Lefty." He gave a quick bow and rang the little bell that hung from a small pole on the wagon. "Lefty Lightfoot. At your service."

"What's the bell for?" Datris asked.

"It scares the desert hounds away. Giddyap!"

Down the sandy road they went.

22

THE CITY of Bone's walls were built from massive stones that would have taken giants to put into place. Behind the walls were spires and balconies of great castles, which could be seen from a mile away. People filed into the city's main gate, seeming like little more than grasshoppers to anyone outside of the great walls.

Lefty Lightfoot led Datris and Gossamer through the gates with little scrutiny. The halfling had a relationship with the soldiers who guarded the walls and entrance into the city.

Gossamer and Datris covered their ears with strips of cloth and drew little attention. They marveled at the breadth of the roads and the gorgeous castles. Every person, rich or poor, was human, and they saw little sign of any other races.

"Is everyone in this a world a human?" Gossamer asked.

"Oh no, not at all. As you can see, I'm a halfling," Lefty said. "But you won't see too many of my kind about. Most of the others shun Bone, but you'll see orcs and dwarves occasionally. The Royals are very particular about who they deal with, but the gates are more open than ever, since the underlings are gone."

"What do you mean?" Datris asked.

"You know, the underlings. Where have you been?"

"Er, we aren't familiar." Gossamer was reluctant to share the information Tatiana had given him when she returned from the Wizard Watch, at least until they knew more about the halfling and could determine whether he could help.

Lefty gave them a funny look as he drove his cart into a huge barn that had a vaulted ceiling. Pigeons nested in the rafters. They dropped to the dirt floor and flew back up again, scattering as the cart approached them. Hundreds of stables were lined up on both sides, but the deteriorating establishment appeared to be mostly abandoned. They ventured toward the darkest area near the back, which was shadowed by the city wall.

Gossamer's nose crinkled at the smell of manure. He slid out of the wagon and helped Lefty unhitch Quickster from his cart. "Can you explain more?"

Lefty led Quickster into one of the stables, which was filled with recently cut hay and a trough of fresh water.

"You know, the underlings. They took over the city, but the Darkslayer ran them off. Don't you know that story?"

"Listen, Lefty," Gossamer said. "A friend of ours passed through here not long ago."

"Oh," Lefty snapped his fingers. "You're trying to find a lost person. It's a big city. They will be difficult to find here." He closed the stable, shutting Quickster inside. "Lucky for you, I have connections. Did this person have pointed ears like the pair of you?"

"Yes, her name was Tatiana. She encountered a man—or a dwarf, rather, when she arrived. Big, with a bushy red beard." Gossamer wrung his hands. "Oh, this is difficult. Would it sound insane to say we're not from this world?"

"That much is clear, but go on about this dwarf fella. Did he have a name?"

"Well, uh, I can't say. But he led her into this city. He thought he knew someone that could help her when she mentioned the underlings."

Lefty went over to his cart and started loading sacks of gear into another stable. Then he seemed to realize what Gossamer had said and dropped them to the ground with a worried expression. "What about the underlings?"

"This is difficult to explain, but the underlings were summoned from your world into our world. We sent them back. Our friend Tatiana was sent here, too, but we summoned her back." Gossamer rubbed his head. "I know this sounds as if I'm out of my skull, but you need to believe me."

Lefty dug his pinky finger into his ear, rummaged through a bag of metal pots and pans, and said, "If your friend is back in your world, how come you're here?"

"We're looking for two others that we were sent to find. You see, the Time Mural we use is still being... er..."

"Tested," Datris filled in.

"Yes, it doesn't function fully, but time is pressing."

Lefty grabbed another sack of goods and set it down inside the stable. "So, there are more of you here."

"Well, they look more like humans. We're elves with pointed ears and more delicate features."

"Elves, huh. Never heard of them." Lefty withdrew some utensils made of solid silver. "The Royals eat this stuff up. Made in the north. I'll get top dollar for them. So, who are you looking for?"

"Dirklen and Magnolia. A man and a woman. They're twins, tall, with blond, wavy hair and light eyes," Datris answered.

"Never seen the like." Lefty scratched his head. "And I know a lot of people."

"They have scars on their cheeks," Gossamer added.

"Oh, you'll see plenty of people with scars around here. You ought to meet my friend Venir. He has them all over. And he's a tall, flaxen-haired man too. But really brawny."

Gossamer fell silent. Venir was the name of one of the

men Tatiana had told him about. She'd spent a great deal of time with them. "Where can we find this Venir? I wish to speak with him."

"Venir? Why?" Lefty grabbed the last pack from his cart and waddled toward the stable. "I'm more likely to find these people than he is. And it's hard to tell where he might be. Tends to wander. But I have close friends in the City Watch. They might know something."

"What about a man named Melegal?"

Lefty dropped his sack, and his jaw dropped. "What did you say?"

23

A MAN WITH A POCKMARKED FACE, tired eyes, and a greasy apron stood behind the bar. "What do you want, half man?"

Lefty stood on his stool, drummed his fingers on the bar, eyed the top shelf, and cheerfully answered, "We'll take a round of your best, Sam." He turned to Datris and Gossamer. "Go ahead. Make yourselves comfortable, friends."

Gossamer gave the run-down tavern, which was named the Drunken Octopus, an uneasy look. It smelled like spilled wine mixed with smoke and many other awful things. Men and women huddled over their tables. Some played cards, while others talked in coarse language. A fireplace burned near the back wall, though its embers were dying.

The stool wobbled beneath him when he sat. Using his hands, he steadied himself.

Sam the barkeep set down a metal goblet for each of them. He filled them to the rim with red wine from a green glass bottle and slammed the bottle down. "Pay up, half man."

Lefty fished some coins out of his string purse and slid them across the bar. "That's enough for two bottles and then some."

Gossamer and Datris each took a sip. Their faces soured, and they set the goblets aside.

"Is there something wrong with your drink?" Lefty asked.

"It burns a little."

Lefty swallowed his and shrugged. "That's more for me, then." He reached over and refilled his goblet with Gossamer's. "Bottoms up."

But before the goblet reached his lips, another man snatched it out of his hands.

"Melegal!" Lefty exclaimed. "Where'd you come from?"

The slender man wore a knit cap smoothed over one side of his face and had eyes like steel. He had salt-and-pepper hair, a gaunt complexion, and a dimpled chin. The sleeves on his golden-yellow silk shirt were rolled up to his elbows, and he wore a plum-colored vest. He drank from Lefty's goblet.

"Nothing had better have happened to Quickster, Lefty," Melegal warned him.

Lefty brushed him off. "He's fine."

Melegal grabbed the bottle, poured, and said, "Then why did you send me a pressing summons? You know what a busy man I am."

"Busy doing what? Sampling other people's wine?" Lefty took the bottle away. "And I'm the one trekking across the Outlands, bringing your junk back so that you can sell it to the Royals at inflated prices. By the way, I need payment."

"Ah, how I delight in selling overpriced junk to those fools. The streams of silver shall flow forever, so long as they live. And you'll see payment after I sample the merchandise." Melegal eased between Lefty and Gossamer. "Sam, a bottle of your worst." He asked Gossamer, "Do you know one side of your hair is different from the other?"

"Melegal, these are the people I want to tell you about. They're friends with that lady you told me about." Lefty snapped his fingers. "What was her name? Tat—"

"Tatiana?" Melegal's face brightened. "Is she here? Venir and Erin ran off with her, and I wasn't so happy about that." He rubbed a finger on the rim of his goblet. "I rather enjoyed her company."

"No, she has returned to her world," Gossamer stated. "We've come searching for others."

Melegal arched an eyebrow. "Like her?"

"No, a man and a woman." He uncovered his ear. "Not like us."

"I can see by your delicate features that you are of the same ilk as her. Disappointing she's not among you." Melegal watched Sam pour a full glass of purple wine, picked it up, and took a pull. "Ah, nothing quite like squeezed grapes for breakfast."

"These are Tatiana's friends Gossamer and Datris. They need our help finding two other friends," Lefty said.

"Well, they aren't our friends," Gossamer added.

"Beg your pardon?" Lefty jumped up on the bar, walked over to Gossamer, and leaned on his shoulder. "Care to explain? Because if they aren't your friends, whose friends are they?"

"They're our enemies."

Melegal gave a razor-thin smile. "Devious. Sounds like something the Royals would do—or I, for that matter. Are you sure you want to find them?"

A huge, mangy black cat jumped up on the bar and lay down by Melegal's hand. The feline's eyes were smoky white. It flexed its eight-clawed paws and yawned.

Melegal stroked the cat's fur and said, "Ah, my dear Octopus, good to see you again."

Gossamer sneezed and continued with his story. "We will be killed one way or the other, but our best chance of survival is to rescue them and buy time."

"And time is pressing," Datris added. "We could be

summoned back at any moment. We'll have to find them quickly."

Melegal smoothed his cap and said, "Bone is a vast place, but nothing ever happens without somebody knowing something. Lefty, have you contacted Georgio and Brak to put out word on the street?"

"No."

"Well, what are you waiting for? Time is pressing. We have friends—*elven* friends—in need." Melegal finished his wine and grabbed the bottle. "I'll put an ear to the ground back at the castle." He patted Lefty on the head and wiggled his bottle. "Don't forget to pay for this." He nodded at Gossamer and Datris. "Nice to meet the both of you. Next time you see her, tell Tatiana hello."

"Yes, and tell your wife, Rayal, hello from me," Lefty replied.

Melegal walked behind the bar and vanished into the kitchen.

With a concerned expression, Datris said, "Do you really think he's going to help us? Or did he just take a free bottle of wine?"

Lefty shrugged. "It's hard to tell, but don't worry. I'm going to help."

24

"WE KNOW exactly who you're talking about," Georgio said. He fanned himself with his cap. "They killed a couple of my men and almost killed us. Been looking for them ever since."

Lefty's friends, Georgio and Brak, had joined them in the Drunken Octopus. They were warrior types, and Brak was huge, towering above Georgio. When he leaned against the bar, it groaned.

Brak rubbed his lantern jaw with a hand big enough to palm a watermelon. "We thought they might be Royals. That would explain how they got the slip on us. We figured they were hiding in one of the castles. Funny —we were going to follow up with Melegal about them."

"How long has it been since you encountered them?"

Gossamer asked. He'd been sipping wine and felt light-headed.

"It's been a few weeks." Georgio blew the foam off a huge tankard of ale and chugged the entire contents. "You're buying, aren't you, Lefty?"

"Anything for my best friend," Lefty said as he flagged down Sam. "Drink all you want. Order food, if you want."

"I'll pass on the food." Georgio let out a long, loud belch. "But there's plenty of room for more ale." He poked Gossamer in the chest. "We'll help you find Dirklen and Magnolia. If anyone can find them, we can." He nudged him with his elbow. "Especially with the help of Lefty." He rubbed his fingers together as if they were cricket legs. "All it takes is a little bit of coin and a dash of persuasion."

"We don't have any money," Gossamer replied.

"Oh, I think you do." Lefty produced the extra gem-studded collar Datris had been carrying. "This ought to cover it."

Datris patted himself down and gave Lefty a wide-eyed look. "You stole that!"

"I only borrowed it. Besides, you have one each on your necks." Lefty twirled the collar on his finger, making a colorful ring in the air.

Datris tried to grab it, but the collar vanished. "Now, now, consider it collateral for services rendered. At least until we can arrange another form of payment. Nothing is free in Bone."

Georgio pulled Gossamer's robes away from his neck, revealing his collar. "Whoa, those must be worth a fortune. Don't let the Royals see them." He covered Gossamer's neck again. "But it's too late to avoid sticky fingers. I'd be sure to keep that on."

"You must understand. We need these collars to return home," Gossamer pleaded. "If we don't make it back, our world's existence is doomed."

Brak leaned forward. "How so?"

"It's a long story. I'd rather you focused on finding Dirklen and Magnolia."

"We like stories. It's been a while since we've heard a good one," Brak said.

Gossamer sighed. The men seemed more interested in being entertained and stealing as opposed to helping them. He felt a hand on his shoulder.

"I'll tell it," Datris offered. "In our world, there is a dragon named Black Frost. His eyeball would fill this room."

The men sat back. Even Sam the barkeep, who was wiping out a mug, seemed interested.

Datris continued, "He drains the magic from other worlds. It makes him bigger and bigger. Once he finishes with our world, there is no reason why he won't try to drain this one."

"He sounds bigger than a castle," Lefty said.

"He is far bigger and every bit as smart."

"How in the world are you going to kill a dragon that big? There is no sword big enough to cut his head off." Brak scratched his head.

They hung on Datris's every word.

"No, there isn't, but if we can cut him off from the source he is feeding from, we surmise that he will shrink back down to the size of a normal dragon again." Datris managed a drink of his wine. "But he rests on top of a temple as big as a mountain and would fill the belly of this vast city you call Bone. It is guarded by hundreds of dragons, each with wings that stretch out from one side of your Royal Roadway to another. His fortress is impenetrable. Hence we must find another way to defeat him, and mastering our Time Mural is the only way we have."

Gossamer couldn't have said it better. Datris told a compelling story and kept it short and simple.

"It's been some time since we've dealt with this sort of trouble." Georgio had his arms crossed. "Sounds to me like duty calls. And I still want a crack at Dirklen and Magnolia. My teeth still tingle from the fire they sent through me."

"Mine as well," Brak stated. He held up his tankard. "It's time to resume the hunt and track those wretches down. When we find them, we'll put an end to them and their wicked plans. They have to go through us if they want to destroy this world. We'll defy the odds. We'll conquer death."

Lefty stood on his stool and said, "We understand, Brak.

You need to keep your speeches shorter, like your father. His inspirations were simple and more elegantly put."

Brak sighed. "Fine." He stretched his tankard over the small group. "Fight or die."

Georgio and Lefty held their cups high. "Fight or die!"

25

SAFE HAVEN

GREY CLOAK SAT on a patch of spongy bright-green moss near the edge of one of the underground lakes. Streak played in the water with some of his brothers and sisters. The dragons splashed one another with their wings, only to submerge beneath the surface and appear again, spraying water from their mouths.

Rummaging through his inside pockets, Grey Cloak found quite a few objects that hadn't been there before. The pockets of his cloak often opened like fish gills as his fingers passed over them, only to close again once his fingers moved on. His pockets had many objects he needed to acquaint himself with after Zanna had had it.

She'd been up to something all those years he'd been turned to stone. Back at the camp, she'd left behind a bandolier of potion vials. *Why did she do this?*

The answer seemed obvious. She was preparing him for the fight to come, but maybe she knew more than she'd let on. Perhaps Zanna knew exactly what he needed to win.

Is she trying to tell me something? I wish I could ask her.

He'd had a difficult time getting to know his mother. She could be frosty sometimes and warm others. It bothered him that he never could tell what she was thinking, leaving him uneasy.

If you can't trust your own mother, who can you trust?

On the far side of the lake, Dyphestive was skipping stones and trying to hit the dragons. Fenora lay beside him, and they were talking. Nath stood with them, hunched over a walking stick, nodding, smiling, and intently watching the dragons.

Grey Cloak checked a few more pockets and removed a blue sapphire the size of an eyeball. "Zooks. The Eye of Enthrallment. How'd she get this?"

He'd traded the gemstone to Batram during an encounter back at Harbor Lake, when they ventured to Prisoner Island. The gem belonged to Drysis, and he'd recovered it when Cinder turned the leader of the Doom Riders into ashes.

Grey Cloak closed his fingers around it, making a fist. *I wonder if I can use its powers.*

He put the gem away then chucked a stone into the lake.

"Ah, I'm tired of waiting around. We need to find a way

to save Talon. I can't wait for Dalsay forever." He started to rise then caught the others looking his direction. But instead of at him, they were looking behind him.

He turned.

A tall woman with long, damp hair and a full suit of dragon armor approached.

Grey Cloak jumped up. "Anya!" He rushed over to her and gave her a strong embrace. "I'm glad to see you!"

"Easy, Grey Garment. You might break me." Her eyes suddenly widened. "Grey Cloak! It's you!" She hugged him back. "I thought you were gone, and when I saw you, it didn't register. Where did you come from?"

"The past, but I'll explain later. Why are you so wet?"

"I came through Lake Flugen." She wrung her hair out. "I fear I have grave news."

"Talon is trapped behind the Flaming Fence," Grey Cloak interjected.

"How'd you know?"

"Dalsay came."

"Ah, I should have known the wizard would beat me here, but that's a good thing. You understand the danger."

A startling dragon call invaded the cavern.

All the dragons in the lake popped out of the water.

Cinder approached with a smile only a dragon could make. "Children, I'm home!" he called.

All of the dragon family came at Cinder like a storm. The water sloshed up on the bank in waves. The dragons bumped horns and nuzzled with their father. The triplets came running from the armory.

"Ho-ho! So glad to see you all, dear children!" Cinder said.

"Dyphestive!" Anya ran, picked him up by the waist, and swung him around. "I've never been so glad to see you. In truth, I'm shocked."

"I'm as happy as you," Dyphestive said.

Streak nudged Anya with his nose. "You didn't forget about me, did you?"

"Lords of Thunder! I didn't recognize you. You're so big, Streak." She hugged his head. "Of course I didn't forget."

Grey Cloak had never seen Anya so jubilant before. Her smile was radiant.

Is that really her, or do I need to pinch myself?

"I don't mean to rain water on the celebration, but have we found a way to rescue Talon from the Nether Realm? It tore me apart to leave them, but I was uncertain what to do. Hence why we went for help."

"Who went for help?" Grey Cloak asked.

"Crane and Tinison wait in Farstick, searching for any aid they can find. I came here, as well as Dalsay, it seems." Anya put her hand on Grey Cloak's shoulder. "I know the situation is perilous, but seeing the both of you gives me hope. We need to return to the Peak of Ugrad and free them. My gut tells me we should go back."

"I'd hoped to hear from Dalsay by now," Grey Cloak

admitted. He glanced at Nath. "When he comes back, you can tell him where we'll be, right?"

Nath nodded. "I'll be waiting, and I'll use the Eye of the Sky Riders to watch over you as well."

"I fear we need to make haste, and the journey back won't be easy," Anya said. "Cinder and I had a difficult time avoiding detection. The Riskers are thicker than hungry rats, and we flew high in the suffocating cold."

"We can handle it," Dyphestive said with a nod. "But I'm going to need a dragon."

26

WIZARD WATCH

ANCIENT LEATHER-BOUND tomes coated in thin layers of dust floated in the air before Dalsay's eyes. The pages flipped right to left at a rapid pace. As one book finished, it floated back into its spot on the library shelf, and another came out.

The Wizard Watch library was a circular room with a wall of shelving running from top to bottom. The old shelves were made from finished oak, polished to a dark shine. Ladders rolled on casters, allowing wizards to reach the top. A balcony wrapped around the room.

Dalsay had no need for such items. In his ghostly form, he floated to where he needed to go. He couldn't touch anything, but with his magic, he still had the ability to command objects. So he pored through book after book, searching for greater understanding of the Flaming

Fence and how to bypass it. The practice was familiar to him.

As a boy, he'd been brought into the Wizard Watch family. He became an able pupil, devouring the knowledge of their craft, and had spent the best days of his life soaking in the knowledge in the archaic tomes. They contained stories that brought history to life and spells that turned minds inside out. Everything the wizards experienced was written down in very vivid detail. Yet the mystery of the Flaming Fence had eluded him.

Hovering near the ceiling, Dalsay scanned the pages, seeking a single nugget of knowledge.

Tatiana had been wise enough to know that the Star of Light would protect her and Talon. She understood the mysteries of how the flaming gate worked. *But without the Star of Light, how can others bypass it?*

Teleportation was an option he'd considered, but based on what he'd been taught long ago, the Flaming Fence guarded against it. A shield needed to be crafted or another Star of Light produced.

A fragment of information caught his eye, and the pages came to a stop. Engrossed, Dalsay read.

Is it possible? Can it be that simple? Is this the only way?

The ancient text slid back onto the shelf.

He sailed across the empty tables and stacks of books. When he was young, the library had been a hive of robust activity between pupils and their mentors. Those days were gone, destroyed by Black Frost and his poison. The mages had been wiped out. Any survivor worth his or her salt had fled. The others who hadn't been killed were minions of evil.

With a sorrowful expression, Dalsay moved into the heart of the tower to an archway with a view outside.

The Black Guard army was still camped around the Wizard Watch, west of the Great River. The Time Mural had been created in the tower and was where the underlings had been defeated.

Dalsay's skin prickled. He didn't normally feel a thing. Nor could he taste or smell, but something tugged at the flesh of his spirit. He passed through the walls and moved into the corridors.

An old enemy, the Scourge, was traveling through the halls.

Honzur the Necromancer. I can't believe it! I thought he'd perished.

Dalsay followed the wicked necromancer, whom he'd crossed on more than one occasion. The Scourge had battled Talon several times, trying to recover the dragon charms. Long ago, he'd been friends with Honzur, but Dalsay had chosen his path, and Honzur had chosen his. They'd been at odds ever since.

Honzur stopped at the entrance to the Time Mural chamber. With a wave of his hand, the slab doorway opened. He entered, and the slab came back down, but not before Dalsay caught a glimpse of the Pedestal of Power, which Gossamer had destroyed.

How can this be?

Dalsay moved inside the wall of the chamber and pushed his face through to the other side, careful to keep hidden from prying eyes. He floated toward the ceiling and had a full view of the chamber.

He'd eavesdropped on Grey Cloak and overheard how Gossamer had planned to rebuild the Time Mural. It appeared that feat had been accomplished. *But what involvement does Honzur have in all this? And why are there no signs of Gossamer?*

Honzur stepped up to the dais and moved behind the pedestal.

A formidable-sized man slouched on one of the pewter thrones with a jug of wine cradled to his chest, napping. His rumbling snores turned into a short snort, waking him. He shook his head, took a sip from his jug, and spotted Honzur. "When did you come back?"

"Moments ago, Commander Covis. Sorry. Did I wake you from your drunken stupor?"

Commander Covis sat up and rubbed his face. "I'm not drunk. I'm bored out of my skull. Why don't you summon them back? I'm sick of staring at the walls in this place, not to mention you."

"The feeling is mutual, but I intend to give Gossamer and Datris ample time to find Dirklen and Magnolia."

Honzur passed his hands over the bowl of gemstones. "But I'm making preparations. It will be soon."

"And what are we going to do if they don't return with Dirklen and his sister?" Covis asked.

"We've talked about this. I have no need for them. We'll kill them. Or *you'll* kill them. That's what I'm keeping you around for." Honzur massaged the ugly scar on his cheek. "Besides, even if Dirklen and Magnolia are returned, we will be rid of Datris and Gossamer. They know too much, and that makes them a dangerous enemy."

Covis settled back into his chair, shut his eyes, and said, "When the time comes, wake me. My blades will be ready."

Honzur loomed over the pedestal, staring intently at the stones. Suddenly, he turned, searching the ceiling.

Dalsay sank back behind the wall, unaware of whether he'd been seen. He moved out of the tower as fast as his ghost form would take him.

I must warn the others. Gossamer's mission is in jeopardy.

27

A SEA of green and a cloudless sky ran for miles in front of Grey Cloak. He rode on Streak with the chill wind in his face, making his hair flap like ribbons. They were high above Arrowwood, where the green pastures were endless. The thread of the Great River could be seen cutting through the thriving land.

Anya and Cinder led the journey north, riding at the top of the *V* formation. Grey Cloak and Streak flew behind their left wing, and Dyphestive rode Smash on the right. They weren't alone either. They were joined by the rest of Cinder's children: Fenora, Bellarose, Snags, Rock, Feather, Slicer, and Slick. The triplets and Chubb had remained behind in Safe Haven with Nath.

The thunder of dragons flew like a flock of geese, cutting the wind resistance and saving their wings.

Cinder took the lead for the longest time. Anya seemed reluctant to have it any other way, but even the great grand dragon needed to fade back and conserve his energy.

"Anya!" Grey Cloak yelled to be heard above the wind.

She didn't turn.

"Anya! Let us take the lead!"

"I think she hears you, but she's not listening," Streak commented. "And I don't think Father is either. He thinks he's protecting us."

"That figures." Grey Cloak caught Dyphestive's gaze and shrugged.

Dyphestive shrugged back.

Grey Cloak smirked. His burly brother on a burly dragon appeared all too formidable. Dyphestive fit on Smash's saddle like a hand in a glove. He'd thought Dyphestive and Rock might have paired up, as Rock was the largest of all the dragons, but Rock had made his independence clear, as always stating, "No riders."

From a few thousand feet above the land, everything below seemed comparatively small and even irrelevant. The Great River was little more than a thread winding through the woodland. Peace that the world on the ground didn't know reigned in the sky.

Before Grey Cloak had departed, he and Nath exchanged their plans. Nath would wait for word from Dalsay. Using the Eye of the Sky Riders, he would also track their location. Of course, everyone knew where they were headed—the Peaks of Ugrad, the Flaming Fence, then the Nether Realm. They were undertaking another impossible mission with the life of Grey Cloak's friends hanging in the balance.

We will save them. I swear it.

Anya stood in her saddle stirrups, leaned over, and peered down. Cinder's head was turned back toward her, and he nodded. With her hair flying in the wind, she pointed downward.

Creatures no bigger than ants flew beneath them. Grey Cloak squinted. It was difficult to tell from the distance, and in the bright sunlight, they could be birds or dragons.

"What do you see, Streak? The sun glare is in my eyes," he said.

Streak dipped his gaze and said casually, "Those are dragons."

"Do they have riders?"

The dragon leaned over. "Looks like it."

"Zooks."

With the journey north halfway over, they'd gone to great lengths to avoid any trouble, but on a cloudless day in the bright sky, they didn't have the natural cover they needed. His eyes followed the riders far below them.

The Riskers were following them, but they didn't rise closer.

"I wonder if they've seen us," Grey Cloak shouted to Anya.

She shrugged and pointed upward.

Cinder led the thunder of dragons higher into the atmosphere.

The Riskers rose with them and started to close the gap.

"It looks like they've seen us," Grey Cloak said. He counted three, each of them a middling. "Must be a Sky Patrol. I don't guess today will be our lucky day." He lifted his voice. "Zora! We're going to have to take action. Stay on course."

"What are you talking about? You stay on course. I'll go after them!"

"Those Riskers' wings are fresh, and they'll be too fast. It's going to take all the speed we have to catch them!"

One of the Riskers broke off from the others and dove toward the surface.

"Thunderbolts! Looks like they're already going after reinforcements." Grey Cloak rose, twisted around, and shouted, "Slick! Slicer!"

The middling dragons peeled off the formation and dove toward the Riskers.

"Dyphestive, switch over to Feather and back them up!"

Streak dropped out of rank.

Grey Cloak said to him, "Get after the one that took off. We have to catch him!"

"You got it, boss." Streak's wings pounded the air. He picked up speed as he dove, folded his wings, and accelerated like a bullet.

Grey Cloak hunched down on Streak, decreasing the air resistance. *Thank goodness I don't get sick anymore.*

The other two Riskers split up.

Bloody Horseshoes.

Slicer and Slick give chase, with Feather and Dyphestive trailing them.

There was no telling how many Riskers might be lurking in the leagues of forest and fields, but one dragon call could draw them all out.

"I've got him in sight, boss. He's diving for the hills," Streak said. "Hold on tight. This little dragon we're chasing is quick."

Streak spread his wings and started to flatten out quickly.

Grey Cloak's stomach jumped.

Ugh! Don't get sick. Don't get sick. Not now.

He lifted his head and peered through Streak's horns. The Risker was making a beeline for a jagged mountain range capped with many tall trees and peaks and disappeared into a chasm cutting through the hills.

"Don't lose him, Streak, or we'll be dead men!"

28

DYPHESTIVE DUG his boots into Feather's stirrups and leaned forward behind her horns. He had to raise his voice to speak. "Can you keep up with them, or am I too heavy?"

"You're big but nothing I can't handle. Besides, I'm faster than my brothers are."

Slick went after one Risker, and Slicer dove for the other.

"Which one do you want me to follow?" Feather asked.

"It's your pick!"

"Slicer it is. He's slower." Feather moved behind Slicer and chased him.

The Risker turned in his saddle and started firing arrows. Glowing projectiles streaked through the sky, skimming over Slicer's body. The Risker dove for the hills with the dragon's tail straightened.

"He's on a path for a getaway. We can cut him off. Put more weight between my shoulders." Feather collapsed her wings.

Dyphestive flattened out the best he could. He felt the wind whistling in his ears as the dragon started to accelerate.

Feather took a sharper angle toward the ground. She caught up with the dragon and dropped beneath him. "Hold on!" She spread her wings and pulled up. Her horns rammed into the dragon's exposed belly.

The dragon bucked.

Slicer zeroed in on the Risker. His back claws clipped the rider's shoulders, spinning him in the saddle.

Fire shot out of the enemy dragon's mouth, coming close to Slicer's tail.

The work had been done. The enemy dragon had to slow, and its opportunity for escape had been cut off. Slicer and Feather flew alongside it.

The Risker nocked another arrow and fired at close range, but Slicer dipped away from it.

Dyphestive grabbed a javelin from an oversize quiver. The enchanted weapon caught fire the moment he touched it, and he hurled it at the Risker. The radiant missile missed by a couple of feet.

"Your aim is awful. Aim for the dragon," Feather said.

"Good idea."

Dyphestive grabbed another arrow just as the Risker prepared to fire. They let loose at the same time.

A bolt of fire sank into the meat of Dyphestive's shoulder. The other dragon pitched forward.

"Well done! You got him under the wing!" Feather cried.

The Risker rode his wounded dragon toward the ground.

"Are you hurt?" Feather asked.

Dyphestive pulled the arrow from his shoulder and cast it aside. "No."

The enemy dragon landed. With bow in hand and quiver slung over his shoulder, the Risker hopped to the ground and started firing at Dyphestive.

Feather veered away.

"What are you doing? Go after them," Dyphestive said.

"I don't want you to get hurt again."

"I'll be fine. Just get me closer to the ground. I'll handle the Risker. You finish off that dragon. And be careful. Watch out for those arrows. They sting."

Dyphestive jumped out of the saddle. He fell twenty feet, hit the high plains grasses, and rolled. As soon as he popped up, another arrow smote him in the chest. "Ugh!"

Streak cut through the chasm, moving from side to side and turning Grey Cloak's stomach into knots.

Hanging on for dear life, Grey Cloak said, "And I thought I was used to this."

"Woo! This dragon is giving me a heck of a time, but I'll get him!" Streak gained speed and narrowed the gap between him and the Risker. His nose almost touched the other dragon's tail. He opened his jaws and snapped at it. "Missed!"

Grey Cloak clung to the saddle, trying to keep his stomach contents down. He broke out in a cold sweat. "Suck it up. You're better than this."

Streak almost had the other dragon by the tail when it ducked under a huge tree that had fallen across the chasm. The Risker went low, and Streak went high, dragging his claws through the branches and jostling Grey Cloak.

"Oof! That didn't feel so good!"

They jetted through the mountain range channels, and a dragon call echoed.

"Uh-oh."

They passed two Riskers hidden in the cliffs. Their middling dragons dropped into the chasm and gave chase.

Grey Cloak barely managed to get the words out. "Streak, we're going to have company!"

"What? I don't remember inviting anyone else to the party." Streak took a quick look over his shoulder. "Oh, more of those guys. You're going to have to handle them."

Grey Cloak turned around in his saddle and grabbed the Rod of Weapons from the javelin sheath. With his stomach bouncing into his chest, he summoned his fire and fought to take aim. "Would it kill you to fly straight for a moment?"

"What?"

"Never mind."

Arrows with tips of flames whizzed through the air and passed Grey Cloak's head. He fired a succession of energy balls from the rod. The spray of energy caught one of the Riskers off guard, and he yanked his reins.

The dragon veered left, but the energy balls struck him and the rider, nearly knocking the man out of the saddle. He clung to the reins as his boots slipped out of the stirrups. The dragon's neck pulled farther left, and they smacked into an outcropping of rock.

"Dead hit!" Grey Cloak cheered. "Ha-ha! Ride the sky!"

Another arrow whizzed straight for his face. Grey Cloak caught it an inch from his eye. He felt the heat coming from it and couldn't believe his eyes. "That was fast." He fed a charge into it and flung it back at the Risker.

The enemy dragon sailed up and over it. It closed in, mouth open and with fire spreading inside of its mouth.

Grey Cloak took careful aim at the dragon's gaping maw and said, "Taste my fire, dragon."

Streak performed a barrel roll, and Grey Cloak fell out of the saddle and toward the rocky depths of the canyon.

The Cloak of Legends billowed, slowing his descent, and he drifted like a leaf while turning.

The pursuing dragon gave chase and bore down on Grey Cloak with a mouthful of flames. They were on a collision course for disaster.

"No!"

29

DYPHESTIVE DUG the arrow out of his chest armor and flung it aside. He'd equipped himself with a vest of dragon scale back in the armory at Safe Haven. The armor hadn't completely stopped the penetration of the fiery arrow, but it had prevented it from piercing deeper. The fire burned, and he bled.

"That's enough of this." Dyphestive drew his forearms in front of him and rushed the enemy.

The Risker nocked another arrow and took aim. The missile streaked through the sky dead on point. It sank into the muscle of Dyphestive's forearm.

He laughed.

Another arrow slipped underneath Dyphestive's defensives and sank into his thigh, but he didn't slow.

The gap between them shrank as Dyphestive sped forward.

The Risker's eyes opened wide, and he tossed the bow aside and went for his sword.

Dyphestive crashed into the warrior before the sharp steel could be unleashed. His first punch knocked the Risker's helmet from his head. *Whop!*

He landed another fierce punch in the man's chest, denting the dragon armor.

The Risker sank to his knees, wheezing. He managed to snake out a dagger and poke at Dyphestive's gut.

He caught the man's wrist and bent it back until it cracked.

"Argh!" Panting, he glared at Dyphestive and said, "You'll die for this!"

"Perhaps but not today." Dyphestive hammered his fist into the side of the man's head, knocking him over like a toppling tower.

Feather and Slicer were engaged in battle with the Risker's dragon. She bit into the dragon's wing and yanked.

Slicer's long claws dug underneath the dragon's scales and ripped them off, exposing the flesh. They wrestled across the grass, a tangle of scales, claws, and powerful limbs.

Feather pulled off part of the dragon's wing then unleashed her flame, searing his body.

The enemy dragon gave a wild, desperate call, like a dying goose.

Slicer sank his teeth into his neck, and Feather turned his body into fire.

Scales and dragon flesh burned. The scorched membrane of skin on the dragon's wings crackled and burned away. His wings flapped futilely. Oily black smoke started to rise, and the stench of death came.

Feather and Slicer walked over to Dyphestive. Their scales had been ripped open in several spots.

Slicer inspected his and said, "Say, beauty marks. I like them."

Dyphestive snapped off the feather end of the arrow in his forearm and pulled it out.

"Ouch, that looks painful." Feather tilted her head and gave him a sympathetic look. "Does it hurt?"

Dyphestive's eyes watered. "Yes, but I've felt worse." He grabbed the arrow in his leg and yanked it out. "Ah! That's better."

Slicer peered at the Risker lying on the ground. "That one's still breathing. I'm going to finish him."

"You don't have to do that," Dyphestive said.

"According to Father, yes I do, or else he'll come back to bite you."

Dyphestive nodded. As much as he hated to see any person suffer, Cinder's wisdom was right. The Risker had chosen the side of evil, and the only way to stop a wicked enemy was to destroy it and not leave a trace.

Slicer leaned over the man and unleashed his flame. The man didn't scream. Instantly, it was over.

"Slick!" Feather said. "Get on, Dyphestive. We'd better go help him!"

The Cloak of Legends had been nothing short of a blessing in Grey Cloak's life, but that day it worked like a curse. He floated toward the earth at an agonizing pace while a dragon flew at him with fire shooting from between his teeth.

Grey Cloak covered himself with his hood and cloak and curled into a ball.

Flames washed over his body. The suffocating heat started to rise, yet no flesh was burned.

Zooks, this is miserable!

The fire died, and he peeked through his hood. The dragon spun in midair and swatted Grey Cloak as if he were a bug. He drifted toward the ledge of the mouth of the canyon, once again floating out of control.

Another arrow whistled past his head.

"Enough with the arrows! Try something original, will you!" He fired a few shots from the Rod of Weapons while trying to float closer to the ledge. His weightlessness made him an easy target, since he was unable to jump, duck, or run.

The branch of a small tree came within his grasp, and he stretched for it.

I can do it! I can reach it!

The Risker had circled around and made another run at him. Fiery arrows led the way, shooting between the dragon's horns and bearing down on Grey Cloak. The missiles sank into the folds of his cloak.

He fired the Rod of Weapons over his shoulder while still reaching for the branch. The gap widened, pushing the branch out of reach.

Grey Cloak kicked the air to spin around, and the dragon rammed his nose into his back and crushed him against the cliffs. His face hit rock, and claws raked down his back. The dragon mauled him.

He jabbed the Rod of Weapons into the dragon's neck and fed it a jolt of energy.

The dragon reared back, wings beating, and hovered.

Grey Cloak gritted his teeth. "I've had enough of this." He launched himself off the cliff and into the face of the dragon.

The Rod of Weapons's sharp point flamed, and he gored the beast between the horns.

The dragon let out a roar, flames spewing, and pitched backward, arching his back. His wings folded. Dragon and rider fell like stones into the rocky jaws of the chasm.

Bones and scales crashed against the jagged stones, and the enemy was heard no more.

Grey Cloak floated downward into the shadows. He was too far from the ledge to catch it.

I really need to find a way to control this fall.

With no wind or aid of any sort, he had no way to avoid the straight drop.

It's going to be one ugly climb getting out. I hope the rest have fared better than I did.

Streak swooshed into the canyon, carrying a Risker crushed in his jaws like a dead rabbit. He dropped the body. "Hey, I've been looking for you."

Grey Cloak floated down into Streak's saddle. "Good. You couldn't have shown up at a better time. Let's go find the others."

30

BISH

SUNLIGHT LEAKED THROUGH THE SHUTTERS, shining on Gossamer's closed eyes. He turned over, and his cot groaned.

An insect buzzed by his ear. He swatted it away and curled up underneath his blanket. He started to drift back to sleep, but sleep hadn't been easy to come by. He'd waited for days to hear word from Lefty Lightfoot and his friends. They were searching for Dirklen and Magnolia, and he'd seen very little of them. But time was pressing. He could be summoned back to his home world at any moment and face certain death.

Splat!

Gossamer sat straight up. Bleary-eyed, he looked around at the apartment Lefty had put them in. The place was small, barely big enough for a pair of cots, a small table, two chairs, and a little iron stove.

"Apologies," Datris said. He wiped his hand on a rag that had green bug guts on it. "But that fly was becoming quite a nuisance. I didn't mean to wake you."

"It's quite all right. I wasn't getting much rest, anyway." He put his feet down on the wood-plank floor. He was still wearing his shoes, since he'd learned his lesson the hard way by walking around the small apartment in his bare feet and getting two splinters. "Is that coffee I smell?"

"Indeed." Datris stood behind a small coal-burning stove, staring at a metal kettle. "I'd hoped to find some tea, but I didn't have any luck. At least not in this part of the city. Would you like a cup?"

"It's the best way to stay awake." Gossamer rubbed his eyes and yawned. He recalled the time when he'd he stayed awake for days on end and never felt the slightest fatigue, though he catnapped a little. But exhaustion had beset him. It had started with his servitude to the underlings. He'd had little time for rest since, and it had all caught up to him.

"Here you go. Careful. It's very hot," Datris said.

"Thank you." He noticed the red rims around Datris's eyes.

Datris was a natural, destined to be a Sky Rider before Black Frost had destroyed them all at Gunder Island. Even his gifts were starting to show wear.

The ceramic mug, almost too hot to touch, warmed Gossamer's hands. He felt that must mean he was alive. He sipped and winced. "I think everything is hot in this world."

Datris rolled up the sleeves of his robe, pulled over a small chair, and sat down with his coffee. "Agreed. But I like it better than the cold. Do you think we could live in such a place as this?"

"We have to return."

"I know, but I can't help but toy with the idea. I've been a slave so long that I hate to relinquish my freedom. I'll take my freedom hot or cold."

Datris had a point. All they had to do was remove the collars and Honzur couldn't summon them back. They would be free.

"Once Black Frost finishes Nalzambor, he'll come for this world and perhaps ours." Gossamer took a longer sip of the black coffee. "You know what we must do."

"I can't help but envision our return to the Time Mural chamber surrounded by a roomful of soldiers with spears pointed at our bellies." Datris leaned over and opened the shutters. "I feel I'm too young to die. I haven't really lived."

Gossamer looked him dead in the eyes. "We're going to find a way to change that. After all, I still feel I have a few good decades left in me too. So don't count us out yet."

Datris nodded. "You know, you've changed."

"How so?"

He shrugged. "You speak differently. Sound tougher." He made a fist. "Hard, like iron."

"I don't know about the rest of me, but my back is as stiff as a rod of iron." He arched back. "Maybe it's the coffee."

Datris giggled. "Could be."

Knock. Knock.

Their attention turned to the apartment door.

Lefty Lightfoot let himself inside with a smile. "Good news. We found them."

Gossamer stood so fast that he spilled coffee on his thigh. "Aah, zeets!" He dabbed his leg with his robes. "Where did you find them? Take us!"

Lefty helped himself to a cup of coffee and said, "Don't burn yourself. I'll take you there. Get some suitable clothing on and get ready." He took a long drink and arched a blond eyebrow. "Not bad. Who made this?"

"I did," Datris admitted. "I added the spices you recommended."

"Not too little and not too much. Just right." Lefty winked. "That's how I like it."

Gossamer and Datris quickly dressed in robes and boots that blended in better with the citizens of Bone, then they hustled to the door.

"Ahem," Lefty said.

They turned.

He held up the pair of ribbons that covered the tips of Datris's and Gossamer's ears. "I told you. Don't leave home without them."

31

GOSSAMER AND DATRIS rode in the back of the mule cart driven by Lefty. They took the Royal Roadway, the main street that connected the north, south, east, and west gates from end to end. Gossamer had never been on a road inside a perimeter before or one that was ten wagons wide. People of all sorts, primarily human, were everywhere. They shopped in the merchant fields and walked the shaded porches in front of the stores.

Women traveled in extravagant carriages. When they stepped out, they wore the most dazzling—and in some cases provocative—clothing he'd ever seen. They wore their wealth proudly, and strapping soldiers in the finest armor escorted them about.

Datris fanned himself with a hunk of wood he'd found

in the cart. His eyes bugged out on occasion, and he turned around several times. "What sort of women are these?"

Lefty chuckled and blew smoke from a tobacco pipe made of horn. "What's the matter? Don't the ladies flaunt themselves in your world?"

"I've never seen the likes of it. Perhaps I've been isolated." He drank from a dried gourd they were using for a water jug. "What about you, Gossamer?"

"I can't say that I've seen women"—he caught a lady being helped out of a carriage—"with legs so long. Er... I mean, I imagine there are places where the women dress in a showy fashion." He turned around. "Lefty, are we close?"

"We've entered the district. We'll meet up with Georgio and Brak in another block or two. In the meantime, enjoy the view. But don't be caught staring. The Royals will arrest you."

Datris gave a puzzled look. "Arrested for what? Staring?"

"Oh yes, they don't like you gawking. I've known people who've had their eyes gouged out for such an offense," Lefty said.

"You jest," Datris replied.

Lefty shook his head, took out his pipe, and blew smoke. He pointed at a beggar sitting on a stool on a street corner. The disheveled man had a cloth ribbon wrapped around his eyes. "He was caught looking too long while a woman was dressing in his shop." He blew out a smoke ring. "Now he begs in front of his shop, which he owns no more, as a reminder of what happens when you look too long."

"Is all of the leadership in this city so vain and callous?" Gossamer asked.

"It used to be worse. Started getting better after the underling menace was dealt with, but the Royals, once humbled, are thriving in their delusions of grandeur once again." He drove the cart off the Royal Roadway and stopped down the next street. "Here we are."

They slid out of the cart and stepped up on the porch.

Lefty handed a street urchin a copper and said, "That's one. Two more when I return, so long as my cart and pony do not leave this spot."

The urchin girl was almost as tall as Lefty. "Word to the Royals, I'll handle it, sire."

Lefty patted her head and said, "I know you will. Feed Quickster a carrot or two, and I'll give a little extra." Left tapped the tobacco out of his long-stemmed pipe and set it on the cart's bench. "Our allies should be close. Come. Follow."

They found Brak and Georgio inside the stables that ran underneath the apartment buildings.

Gossamer sneezed.

Several soldiers from the City Watch popped up from their hiding places.

Georgio gave Gossamer an irritated look. His shoulders

were hunched. "Do you think you can keep that under control? We're trying to spy your friends. No need to alert them and the entire town of our whereabouts."

"Apologies. The smell of manure gets me."

Gossamer rubbed his nose. He moved beside Georgio, who'd concealed himself behind the stable wall. He was spying on the building on the other side of the street, opposite of the building where they'd left Quickster.

"I don't see them," Gossamer said.

"That's because they're inside that tavern," Georgio replied. He jabbed his finger toward the building.

The painted sign above the establishment read The Chimera's Claw. Unlike the tavern where Gossamer dwelled, that one was well built with the finest materials. The entrance door was oak. A man in an apron stood outside, polishing the door fittings.

"Your friends are in high company, it seems," Georgio said.

"What do you mean?"

"That tavern is where Royals spend their time. It's where the merchants that wish to do business with them come." Georgio scratched the back of his neck. "Merchants aren't allowed in the castles. Only Royals allowed. Not ordinary citizens, aside from the servants."

"How do you know they're inside?" Gossamer asked.

"We took a wild guess and picked this one out of a hundred other taverns."

"Oh."

Georgio slapped him on the back. "I'm pulling your leg. We caught them going inside yesterday and haven't seen them come out."

"I don't mean to offend, but what if they slipped out?"

Georgio shook his head. "I have a lot of men. And we have eyes on the back too. They aren't going to slip past us. Besides..." He pointed at the third-story window.

Magnolia sat there, running a comb through her hair.

"That's our girl, isn't it?"

Gossamer nodded.

A moment later, Dirklen stuck his bitter face out the window.

Gossamer crouched but peeked over the sill.

Dirklen scanned the streets and closed the shutters.

"He's gone," Georgio said.

"Well, aren't you going to arrest them?" Gossamer asked.

"Can't do it. Whoever is in that tavern is a guest of the Royals. Meaning they're out of our jurisdiction. But once they come out, they're all ours."

"So, what do we do?"

Georgio took off his hat, fanned himself, and put it back on. "Either we wait, or we find a way to flush them out."

A renewed sense of urgency overcame Gossamer when he met eyes with Datris. "We have to flush them out."

"All right, then. We'll need a plan."

32

"Do you think you can refrain from basking in the sun at the window for the rest of the day?" Dirklen paced the room, hands behind his back. "Or do you want to be found, quartered, and killed?"

Magnolia rolled her eyes. She moved over to the vanity in the well-furnished room, sat down, and resumed stroking her comb through her hair. "They won't find us with so many people in this city. They're like flies, buzzing all around. I think we're safe. Besides, our Royal allies are looking out for us."

"Oh yes, the Royals, all of which we've known a couple of weeks." He flopped down onto a small sofa made of crushed velvet and stretched his arms out over the back. "We're close acquaintances, aren't we?" He blew away a strand of hair hanging over his eye. "They'll cut our throats the moment they have no use for us. Do you really think your flirting is going to return us to our home world?"

"It's working so far." She smiled at herself in the mirror. "The Royals think they're manipulating me, but I am manipulating them. It's fun. Besides, do you have any better ideas on how to return home?"

"No, but I can use the same tactic that you have. I'll toss my hair and bat my eyelashes at the next noblewoman who strolls in here. Perhaps she'll be a sorceress who travels between worlds. With a twitch of her lips, she'll transport us home."

"Mock all you wish, but I'm finding ways to enjoy myself."

"I'll enjoy myself again when we're home and Grey Cloak is dead."

A heavy knock on the door startled both of them.

"You can answer it. I'm sure it is the Royal friend of yours."

Magnolia tightened the belt on her silk robe, walked across the floor barefooted, and said, "Be cordial, if you please. Royal Lord Anton is here to help us."

"I have no doubt about his ulterior motives. And you should be fully dressed."

"Perhaps you should be the one to answer the door, then."

Dirklen grabbed a pillow and made himself comfortable on the sofa. "Sorry, but I wasn't expecting any company."

Magnolia cracked the door open. "Royal Lord Anton, what a pleasure to see you again."

He bowed and said, "A pleasure to see you again, too, Magnolia." The handsome Royal was about her age, his hair and beard were neatly trimmed, and he wore a tunic of the finest materials, but he was not very tall. "I can see you're in your gown. Perhaps I should come back later."

She opened the door wider and said, "No, not at all. After all, we were expecting you, and I should have been fully dressed by now. I admit I've been lazy this morning. I didn't feel like taking my robe off. It's so comfortable."

Dirklen rolled his eyes, but he sat up as Lord Anton entered the room. He tipped his chin at the man, who seemed a little surprised to see him.

Anton strolled over and offered his hand. "Well met, Dirklen. I hope you're comfortable in your accommodations."

Dirklen stood, looked down at Lord Anton, and replied, "We're grateful for the House of Anton's hospitality. After all our troubles, the grace you've shown to us could not have come at a better time." He clutched his heart. "We were in a pit of despair."

"I can't imagine the horrors you faced when those brigands took you. Your escape is miraculous."

Dirklen rubbed his cheek. "And we have the scars to show for it."

The moment Lord Anton turned his attention back to ogling Magnolia, Dirklen's charming smile vanished. Magnolia had concocted a story about how they were Royals traveling from the City of Three, overtaken by brigands on their journey to the City of Bone. The smitten Lord Anton bought it hook, line, and sinker. He'd been trying to aid them, Magnolia in particular, ever since.

Magnolia flipped her hair over her shoulder and asked, "Lord Anton, have you been able to find a mage for us?"

"Certainly. After all, I'm from a very powerful house with the finest services at our disposal. As a matter of fact, I come bearing good news as well. I've made arrangements for you to meet with the mage this evening."

"Here?" Dirklen asked.

"Yes. This very spot. As I've said, my house has everything a man can offer. This mage has renowned abilities and owes our house many favors. I'm confident the brigands who accosted you will be located, and all of your precious goods will soon be found."

"That's wonderful, Lord Anton." Magnolia threw her arms around the little man and gave him a firm hug, cracking his back.

"Oh my!" a wide-eyed Lord Anton exclaimed. Once she broke off the embrace, he said, "This is cause for celebration. I have some business to attend to, but I'd delight in your company for lunch later this afternoon, Magnolia."

"I will be there," she said.

Lord Anton kissed her hand. "You honor me." He nodded at Dirklen and departed.

Dirklen flopped back down on the sofa. "Fantastic. I can't wait for the wedding and the day you deliver the offspring of the little goat man."

Magnolia laughed. "You might think him amusing, but I find Lord Anton to be cute and charming."

"You enjoy any man that slobbers all over you." He lay back down and closed his eyes. "Do you think this mage will pan out?"

"I don't know, but we'll find out soon enough. Now, if you'll excuse me," she said as she stepped into the bedroom. "I have a lunch to get ready for. And it will be one little Lord Anton will never forget."

33

FARSTICK

SERGEANT TINISON LOADED a barrel into Crane's wagon. Sweat beaded on his forehead. He shoved the barrel against the side of the wagon and started to tie it down. "That's the last one. I think we have everything you wanted."

Crane finished getting Charro into her harness. He climbed onto the bench and replied, "Good. Let's go then."

"I don't understand why we're going to Black Stow," Tinison said as he climbed into the back of the wagon. "We should stay close to the Black Foothills, shouldn't we?"

"Farstick is dried up. We've been here over a week, and I haven't made a single connection with the Brotherhood of Whispers. Now that Sasha is dead, the town has gone silent. And the longer we stay here, the more out of place I feel."

"I know the feeling. I swear every Black Guard we pass is staring at me." Tinison settled into his seat by the barrels and groaned. "Ah, my back. Why'd we buy all this grain, anyway?"

Crane flipped his horse whip, and Charro started forward. The wagon jerked and headed out of the barn.

It was another cold day in Farstick. Snow flurries were coming down. Charro headed toward the west gate, which led to the road to Black Stow.

Tinison kept his head down, but he felt eyes all over him, though he didn't catch anyone staring except the occasional Black Guard soldiers they passed. And there certainly weren't any waves goodbye.

"Do you want to climb up front?" Crane asked.

"I don't mean to sound like a softy, but I'm not ready to rise yet. Sometimes it feels like that wind will cut me in half." He patted a leather flask. "Good thing we brought plenty of this hooch. It's the only thing good in Farstick, as far as I'm concerned."

Craned nodded. "Agreed. Lucky for us, every town has a special hooch to help get us through."

The wagon bounced and jostled over the rough road and made its way under the west gate, where a bleak sky over the open plains waited.

Tinison looked back. "I won't miss it, but I don't think Black Stow is going to be any better. Ugrad is a cheerless place."

A squad of Black Guard horsemen passed under the west gate and followed them down the road from a distance.

Grabbing the wine flask, Tinison said, "Crane, I don't mean to sound paranoid, but we might be being followed."

Crane turned his head over his shoulder and asked, "Why do you say that?"

"A Black Guard quartet is riding behind us, and a chill fell over my shoulders." He pulled the cork out of the flask and drank. "What do you think?"

"I think someone has been watching us, but I don't know who. That's why I wanted to head to Black Stow, away from the action. Draw them off. And who knows—we might find more allies down there."

"Good, because we're running out of allies."

The wagon wheels rolled from dawn to dusk. Tinison lost sight of the Black Guard, only to see them appear time and again.

Crane led the wagon off the road, into a clearing in the woodland.

"What are you doing? Shouldn't we keep going and lose them? Have your magic horse spin these wheels." Tinison drew his sword. "I have a feeling they're here to kill us."

Crane climbed out of the wagon. "Probably."

Tinison blanched. "What do you mean, 'probably'? They're coming to kill us, and you want to make camp."

Crane laid a hand on Tinison's shoulder, and with a

twinkle in his eye, he said, "Let them think they have the jump on us. We'll be ready."

"I don't see how."

"Help me pick up some sticks. We need a fire."

Tinison shuffled around the area, picking up sticks. His back was as tight as a bow string, and he ground his teeth.

How can he be so calm about all of this? Those soldiers are following us.

The campfire did little to ease his tension. Covered in a blanket, he squatted in front of the fire and warmed his hands.

Crane sat across from him, uncharacteristically quiet, and nibbled a strip of dried beef.

A horse who wasn't Charro snorted.

Tinison grabbed his sword, which had been lying on the ground beside him.

Four men on foot appeared from the darkness, surrounding them. They were Black Guard in full gear, helms and all, but their swords remained sheathed.

"We saw your fire and thought we might join you. Apologies if we startled you," one of the soldiers said in a weathered voice. "I'm Monduke."

"Can't you make your own fire? Why share ours?" Tinison asked.

"No need to be impolite, Tinison. Any members of the Black Guard are welcome in our camp." Crane spread his arms. "Please, sit." He offered them a flask. "Drink if you thirst, Monduke."

Tinison's blood warmed. The soldiers' eyes were fixed on him.

What is Crane doing? Why did he use my name?

The leader of the Black Guard held his hands out over the fire. "It's going to be a cold night. Cold for some, more so than others. Isn't that right, Crane?"

"You get used to it," Crane answered.

Tinison's grip on his sword tightened. "How do you know his name?" he asked.

Showing a mouthful of tobacco-stained teeth, Monduke replied, "Because I know everything." He gave a quick nod.

The soldiers drew their weapons and attacked.

34

TINISON DIDN'T KNOW what Crane was up to, but the man had clearly betrayed him. Before the Black Guard could close in on his position, he dashed for the woodland.

"Get after him," the leader said. "Cut him down."

Tinison jumped over a fallen tree and raced into the darkness. Twigs and fallen branches snapped under his feet. He plowed through thatches and bushes.

I sound like a bull charging through here! I need to hide. Hide and strike. You're a member of the Honor Guard. You can handle them.

He braced his back against a tree, tried to quiet his frosty breath, and listened.

"Spread out, men. He can't be far. Once you get an eye on him, give a yell." The soldier cleared his throat. "Come on out, Tinison. Make this easy on yourself. Come out of the cold and die like a man."

Footsteps crunched across the ground. They were getting closer. Tinison held his sword tight to his chest and kissed the cold blade.

I can take one of them, possibly two, but can I get all three in time? One way or the other, one of them is going to the grave with me.

His mind raced, and he couldn't shake the thought of Crane's betrayal. He'd been thrown completely off guard.

Why would he do this? Why now? Why me?

A soldier cried out, and someone fell to the ground.

"Harvin, is that you?" the leader asked. His question was met with silence. "Franco, do you have eyes on Harvin?"

Franco replied, "No, Kalser, no sign of—who are you? *Urk!*"

"Harvin! Franco! What's happening?"

Tinison peeked around the tree and spotted Kalser hiding with his back to a tree.

The Black Guard called again, "Franco! Harvin! Respond to me!"

Death lingered in the air. With his hair standing on end, Tinison felt it.

Someone or something is killing these men. And it isn't me.

Kalser started coming his way. With an unseen enemy

in their midst, he wasn't sure what to do, but the hardened soldier in him took over, and he stepped out in full view. "What's the matter? Lose your men?"

Kalser sneered. "I know it wasn't you who killed them. My men are more than a match for a scrappy little Honor Guard."

"You seem to know a lot about me."

"That's because we know everything." Kalser put a two-handed grip on his sword. His eyes darted from side to side. "Who's helping you? Where are they? Come out!"

"What's the matter? Don't like the odds against you?"

"Oh, I can handle you all by myself."

"If that were the case, why'd you come with two men?"

Kalser moved closer. "It's how we operate." He jumped forward and thrust.

Tinison parried the sword strike and punched his dagger into the man's chest.

Kalser wheezed.

"You didn't see that coming from this scrappy little soldier, did you, Kalser?" As the man died, he lowered him to the ground. "Never underestimate the Honor Guard."

Tinison found the other Black Guards. They were both dead. Their bodies were contorted, eyes wide, and not a drop of blood showed.

What in the world did this?

He crept back toward camp with sword and dagger in

hand, fully ready to confront Crane and the old man's bizarre betrayal.

But what if the monster lurking in the darkness took Crane out already? He deserved it for turning his back on me.

Tinison spied the camp from the edge of the Woodland.

Monduke lay dead on the ground with his arms up, his crooked fingers twisted toward the air.

Crane hadn't moved from his spot. He was speaking with a mysterious person wearing a full cloak and a jovial smile.

The person in the cloak turned Tinison's way and nodded him over.

Weapons bared, Tinison marched into camp. "What sort of treachery is this, Crane?" His breath was steaming. "You sent assassins to kill me?"

With a shocked expression, Crane replied, "Of course not. That wasn't the plan. But introductions first. I want you to meet a dear friend of mine."

The cloaked figure turned.

"Tinison, meet Zanna. Zanna Paydark."

When Zanna dropped her hood, Tinison's jaw fell along with it. The dark-haired elven woman was a striking beauty. He swallowed the lump building in his throat and said, "Are you the one who killed those men?"

"Nothing gets by you, does it, Sergeant Tinison?" she asked in a smooth voice.

"Why didn't you kill the last one?"

Zanna shrugged. "I thought I'd save him for you." She winked at him. "I knew you could handle it."

His cheeks warmed. He sheathed his blades, stuck out his chest, and said, "I would have downed them all if you hadn't come around. But how did you kill them?"

Crane stood with a moan. He arched his back and said, "Zanna is a Sky Rider. And she's Grey Cloak's mother."

"Oh." Tinison managed to tear his gaze away from Zanna and fix his attention on Crane. "Would you care to explain to me what happened? I thought you turned on me."

Crane gave a slight bow. "I apologize. I came across Zanna back in Farstick. She knew we were being watched, and we devised a plan to flush our enemies out. This was the rendezvous point. It will buy us time to slip our enemies."

"Why didn't you let me in on it?"

"We didn't want to risk tipping our enemies off. They're clever, and we feared another changeling might be among them. Fortunately, there wasn't."

"I don't play that way, Crane." Tinison poked the man in the chest. "Don't do me like that again. I deserve better."

"I won't."

"So, what's the plan now?"

Crane took a small box out of his travel sack and

opened the lid. A small green dot moved inside a bed of sand. "Now we track down Grey Cloak."

"He's alive?" Tinison asked.

Zanna answered, "Alive and very disappointed in his mother."

THE BLACK FOOTHILLS

THE DRAGONS DRANK from a mountain stream, and Grey Cloak paced the bank. It had been a long flight from Safe Haven. They'd survived one encounter and made it across the Green Hills without another. They waited.

Grumbling, Grey Cloak said, "Dalsay should be here by now. How much longer do we have to wait?"

Dyphestive called from the camp, "Grey! We have company!"

Grey Cloak ran back to the camp as fast as the fleetest deer with the Rod of Weapons's tip glaring.

The apparition of Dalsay stood among the small group, and a newcomer was with him—a tall, strapping fellow carrying a wood-axe.

Grey Cloak doused his flame. "You didn't have to make it sound as if we were being invaded, Dyphestive."

"Sorry, but I knew you were eager for his arrival."

"Apparently, he was," Anya said.

"Allow me to introduce West. He will guide you to the Flaming Fence," Dalsay said solemnly.

"I thought you were going to guide us," Grey Cloak said.

"I would go along for the journey, but I fear I have come upon more pressing matters."

"Such as?"

Dalsay replied, "When I traveled back to the Wizard Watch, I made a startling discovery. Honzur the Necromancer has taken over the Time Mural. On Black Frost's order, he sent Gossamer and Datris back to Bish to find Dirklen and Magnolia."

"*What?*" Grey Cloak exclaimed. "How could this have happened?"

"Black Frost is wise. He must have suspected something and was quick to make changes. It is clear he doesn't want Gossamer and Datris back alive. I must return and find a way to help them, or all of our efforts will fall into ruin."

Grey Cloak wanted to pull his hair out. "This can't be happening. If Gossamer and Datris don't send Zanna back in time, we're all doomed."

"I understand the enormousness of the consequences. You must have faith that I will find a way to see it through."

Grey Cloak jabbed the rod into the dirt. "If you don't come with us, how are we supposed to cross through the Flaming Fence without a wizard?"

"I scoured the Wizard Watch's archives with little success, but I did discover this sliver of hope. Pure-blooded naturals can walk through the flames, but it will be painful if not purifying."

Anya laughed. "Oh, this is getting better and better."

"Without the Star of Light, I can offer no other way," Dalsay said. "The flames are designed to destroy what is within, not what is without. That's why the evil ones cannot escape. But a natural with true intentions can."

"You're telling us we can walk through the fires, and our gear won't go up in smoke?" Grey Cloak asked.

"In theory." He glanced at Anya. "But your armor will become awfully hot."

"I won't wear it, then," she said. "I have to admit the thought of my flesh cooking doesn't sit well with me."

"What are we going to do? Go in without our equipment? Didn't you say there are thousands of them in the Nether Realm?" Grey Cloak asked.

"The last thing you want to do is engage a throng of bitter people. You will not be able to overcome them. Not to mention that there are giants and dragons within as well. Use a more subtle tactic. Find the Star of Light. Utlas, the speaker, will certainly have it close. If you can get the star to Tatiana, she will provide a way out for the others."

"What about the Dragon Helm?" he asked.

"Take what you can, but what is more important?

Saving your friends or retaining the Dragon Helm?" Dalsay asked. "You might have a very hard choice to make."

"Thanks, Dalsay, but know this—we're getting the Dragon Helm and our friends." Grey Cloak turned to West. "So, Mountain Man, are we ready?"

West offered his hand. "At your service. I'm ready to go."

Grey Cloak received his strong grip. "So are we."

As Dalsay started to fade, he said, "I'll return when I can. Dragon speed to you all."

When he vanished, a horse-drawn wagon pulled by a beautiful horse rolled into camp.

"Crane!" Dyphestive called. He rushed over to the man, helped him out of the wagon, and gave him a strong embrace. "I've been overjoyed since I heard you were alive. And now to see you in the flesh! Exhilarating!"

"Easy, now," Crane said, his face beet red. "My bones aren't made of iron like yours."

Dyphestive set him down and messed up his hair. He sought out Tinison and bumped forearms with him. "Good to see you, Sergeant!"

"You, too, Dyphestive," Tinison replied. "If I had an acre of land for all the ghosts I've seen come back to life, I'd be a wealthy man."

Dyphestive slapped Tinison on the shoulder, knocking him off balance.

"Hello, Dyphestive."

Grey Cloak turned his attention away from Crane when

he heard the sound of Zanna's voice. She approached his brother with a warm smile on her face.

"Zanna?" Dyphestive wore a confused expression.

She stepped toward him, but he backed away.

An awkward silence fell over the camp.

Crane broke it. "Look at this—a family reunion."

All eyes were on Zanna, who didn't appear to be uncomfortable at all.

"What are you doing here, Zanna?" Grey Cloak asked.

"I want to help."

Grey Cloak crossed his arms and asked, "And how do you propose to do that? Are you going to turn us all to stone again? Or did you have another variety of torment in mind?"

"I know what you've been through. I can explain." She gave him a pleading look. "If you'll permit me."

"Come along, then," he said with a glare. "After all, the Flaming Fence might be the perfect fit for you."

36

BISH

"Interesting," Georgio said. "It looks like Royal Lord Anton is back. He's been a busy boy lately, it seems."

Gossamer stood and brushed straw from his back. They'd been spying from the stuffy, smelly barn all day, with the constant company of flies that kept him busy. He swatted another away from his face. "What do you mean? Who is he?"

"A little runt of a Royal. He's a member of a formidable house but on the butt end of the pecking order." Georgio sniffed. "He's come and gone three times today. That's odd."

"So, you know him?" Gossamer asked.

"Oh, we've dealt with him before. Haven't we, Brak?"

In his low voice, Brak replied, "He's difficult to forget. A petty little man who takes advantage of his status and flaunts it like gold." He peered down at Gossamer. "He tried to have me thrown into the dungeon for looking at him wrong. But I think it's because I'm so tall that it scares him."

Lefty chuckled. "I remember that. I'm the one who talked him out of it." He was lying on a bed of straw, puffing smoke from his pipe. "I don't know why he's ashamed of his height. It's an advantage."

"Look here," Georgio said.

A black horse-drawn carriage pulled in front of the Chimera's Claw, blocking the view of the front door. A gaunt driver dressed in black ambled out of his seat and vanished on the other side of the carriage.

The carriage rocked, and the door opened and closed.

A moment later, the driver climbed back into the wagon and drove away. The front door of the tavern remained closed.

"I didn't see anything. Did you?" Georgio asked Brak and Lefty.

Lefty was lying on his belly. "I didn't see any boots. It's as if the person were a ghost or something else."

"Perhaps it was another Royal being dropped off," Datris suggested.

"Royal carriages boast their banners. They love to put on a show. But that wagon was as black as a funeral carriage but without such a mark." Georgio scratched his head. "Someone went inside, and they didn't want anyone to know about it."

Lefty brushed off his vest. "I can get a closer look at that carriage, if you wish."

Brak sniffed. "Do you smell that?"

"It wasn't me," Georgio said.

"That's not what I'm talking about." Brak's nostrils widened. "It smells of wet bark and incense."

"A mage?' Georgio put on his hat.

"Perhaps," Brak answered.

"Well, I'm going to find out." Lefty nodded and slipped across the street.

Georgio elbowed Gossamer and said, "Don't worry. He'll find out what it is. He's really good at spying."

"So, mages don't spend time in taverns?" Gossamer asked. "That isn't ordinary."

"Not at all. Mages rarely show themselves."

Dirklen and Magnolia were joined by Lord Anton and his guest, a tall, slouched person covered from head to toe in pitch-black robes.

"Allow me to introduce Mistress Alania from the Guild of Mages," Lord Anton said politely. "My house has been acquiring her services for a very long time. She is the finest in her craft. You'll see."

"Welcome, Mistress Alania," Dirklen said. He tried to get a look at her face, which was hidden under her hood.

The woman's hands were also hidden in her sleeves, and her robes covered her feet. He figured her for an old hag, dragged from the cellars and alleys. When she lowered her hood, he faced an entirely different picture. His eyebrows rose. "Welcome indeed."

Mistress Alania was beauty with silken black hair tied back in many braids. The heavy stare of her simmering eyes soaked Dirklen and Magnolia in. Tiny tattoos dotted her elegant cheeks like freckles. Her skin was smooth and as white as ivory, not darkened by the suns like ordinary men.

"It is my pleasure to meet both of you," Mistress Alania said in a sultry voice. "I can see you're not from here." She touched the scar on Dirklen's cheek. "That pains you, doesn't it?"

He cleared his dry throat. "It does."

"I can take your pain away." She glanced at Lord Anton. "My lord, this process is very intimate. Will you allow us some privacy while I work my craft?"

Lord Anton pulled a chair back from the table for her. "It won't be any bother at all. I have colleagues downstairs whom I've planned to join. And I'll see to it you aren't disturbed."

Mistress Alania caressed Lord Anton's face and gave him a soft kiss on the cheek. "Thank you, my dear Lord Anton." She sat down.

Once Lord Anton had departed, she said to Dirklen,

"Would you be a dear and secure the door? As Lord Anton mentioned, it is very important that we don't have any interruptions."

When Dirklen didn't move, Magnolia locked the door and joined her brother and Lady Alania at the small dinner table. She knitted her brow at her brother.

He caught his sister's warning glance and tore his gaze away from the enchanting seductress. "You've been in the service of Anton's family for a long time?"

"I have," Lady Alania said in a voice more like a purr. "They have very demanding but trivial needs. My abilities are often wasted on them, but your story intrigued me when Lord Anton brought it to me."

"How so?" Magnolia asked.

"I knew it was a lie." She offered them both a devilish smile. "But that's what made me curious. But don't worry. Lord Anton doesn't suspect your deceit. Clearly, he is smitten with you, Magnolia. Well done."

Magnolia placed her elbows on the table. "But you do intend to help us?"

"I will." Mistress Alania grabbed their hands. "Once I know your entire story."

Dirklen's limbs became like wood. Fire shot through his blood. Across from him, his sister's expression was one of horror. A floodgate opened, and his memories poured through him. He screamed in his mind.

37

DIRKLEN SHOOK his head and blinked. A cold wave washed over him.

Magnolia rubbed her eyes. Sweat beaded on her forehead, and her lips trembled.

In a daze, Dirklen asked, "What did you do to us, witch?"

"Easy now, mighty one," Mistress Alania said as she rubbed his icy hands in her warm palms. "No harm came to either of you. I soaked in your thoughts and learned much about your journey. My method is much faster than having you take the time to explain it."

"You read our thoughts?" Magnolia pulled a dagger out. "Who does such a thing?"

"I apologize. I took you by surprise, but I think it will be worth it. After all, you're trapped on our world, and you need to find your way home." Mistress Alania released Dirklen's hands and reached into her robes. "I believe I can help."

"You'd better, or trying will be the last thing you do," Magnolia warned her.

"Easy, sister. I sincerely believe she's trying to aid us," Dirklen said.

"Of course you would. You're smitten."

"There's no need for that sort of talk." Dirklen eased back in his chair. "I want to see how this plays out. What did you learn about us, Alania?"

Alania placed a small leather sack on the table and started to untie the strings. "I know your world is another world away. Gapoli is the name. You serve a mighty ruler, a dragon, as black as the night. You were betrayed by an acquaintance inside a great tower that hosts a doorway. I would so love to visit another world like yours. I've dreamed of such things."

Magnolia stuck her dagger into the table. "There is only room for my brother and me."

"I see." Mistress Alania withdrew a stone from the sack. It had four level sides and was shaped like a pyramid. Runes were engraved in the faces, and the edges were smoothed over. She stretched out a finger. The tips of her black nails were painted gold. "This is the Stone of Many Faces. It will aid us. We will need to find another gate—an attachment to your world in this one."

Magnolia stiffened and said, "I think that much is obvious."

"Yes, it should be. I know there is magic in both of you. I felt it the moment I entered the room. You are extraordinary people." Mistress Alania eyed Magnolia's dagger. "May I?"

"For what?" Magnolia asked.

"I need something from your world to find a link from this one. Do you know of any others that have traveled between our worlds?"

"The underling Lords Verbard and Catten made quite a stay," Dirklen said.

Mistress Alania gasped. "Did you say underlings?"

Perplexed, he glanced at Magnolia. "Yes. Why does that surprise you?"

"The underlings were eradicated long ago. Where are these underlings now?"

He shrugged. "I believe here, but I can't be certain."

"And there was a woman from our world, Tatiana, who visited here as well," Magnolia offered.

"She returned?" Mistress Alania asked.

"Indeed."

"How so?"

"A collar around her neck. She was able to be summoned back by the underlings, who controlled the Time Mural at the time," Dirklen replied. "Can you help us?"

Mistress Alania took Magnolia's dagger and said, "Every morsel of information you feed me will increase the possibility now that I have an object to look for." She closed her eyes and began to chant rhythmically.

The runes engraved in the stone pyramid started to burn with radiant light. Each side was a different shade, casting colorful shadows across the room.

Gripping the dagger in both hands, the sorceress swayed back and forth and from side to side. Her head rolled loosely on her neck, and her murmurings became louder. She let out a shocking cry.

Colors sprayed out of the stone, and a vision formed in the air above the pyramid's tip.

Mistress Alania's chanting stopped, and she opened her eyes. "I feel your world. It's here. It is close," she said in a loud whisper. "Gaze into the image. Do you see it?"

A sphere took shape above the table. Streets and buildings formed and sharpened into a crystal-clear view.

"It looks like the City of Bone," Magnolia commented.

"It is," Mistress Alania said. She swayed back and forth over the table. "Your gateway is closer than I ever would have imagined. I can feel it in my bones." She passed her hand by the stone.

The pyramid began to rotate slowly.

"I can see the streets as if I were walking them myself," Dirklen said. He spotted the entrance to the Chimera's

Claw. "It's a vision of this tavern. What good will that do us, Alania?"

"No," she said in a hushed voice. "Look closer."

The image turned to face the stables across the street and moved in. Many members from the City Watch were gathered inside, keeping their bodies out of full view.

"They have found us. They're spying on us," Magnolia said with a worried look. Georgio's face appeared, and she gasped. "Is this a trap, witch? This gateway is toward our doom."

"No, that's not it. Look deeper. I swear it is there, right at the tips of my fingers." Mistress Alania wiggled her fingers like falling rain. "There. Look."

The image zoomed in on another man, who didn't match the others. He sat on a pile of straw with his face buried in his hands. A strip of cloth was wrapped around his head. One side of his long, unkempt hair was black, and the other side was white like cotton. His robes were frayed but checkered in black and white.

Dirklen tilted his head. "It can't be."

The man lifted his head and spoke to another man. There was no mistaking his elven features.

"Gossamer!" Dirklen rose from the table with his eyes fixed on the man's image. "How can this be? Why is he here?" He peered at the sorceress. "Is this here? Is this now? Or a shade of what is to come?"

"It's now," she assured him.

"Look, brother, on his neck. I see a collar," Magnolia said. "And that's Datris from the temple. He's wearing a collar as well." Her face brightened. "They've come for us! We're saved!"

Dirklen moved to the window and peeked through the shutters. The huge man, Brak, wasn't hiding very well, and his big face poked out of the stables. "If we're saved, then what are they waiting for? What sort of treachery is afoot? I don't like this."

38

THE PEAKS OF UGRAD

"A LITTLE HELP?" Streak asked. His body was wedged inside the narrow walls of the cave.

Grey Cloak sighed. "Didn't I tell you not to come? West said you might be too big. You aren't as small as you used to be."

"I'm a dragon. We're used to squeezing through tight places." Streak looked through his legs. "Someone give me a shove back there. Ow! Hey, who's butting me with their horns? I know it was you, Slick!"

The dragons trapped on the other side of Streak giggled.

Dyphestive grabbed one of Streak's claws and started pulling.

Streak wiggled.

West stroked his beard and said, "I never imagined a

journey into the Cavity of Chaos escorted by dragons. I find it amusing."

"Are we very far from the fence?" Grey Cloak asked.

"The long part of the journey is over. We're on the cusp of the final descent."

"Good." Grey Cloak searched for a spot to sit down. It seemed like they'd been walking forever through the hills, which were covered in ice. The caverns offered little comfort. He sat down.

"You can't avoid me forever," Zanna said when she caught his eye. "We need to bury the hatchet."

"No one trusts you, Zanna. Not even Streak or my brother, who is extremely trusting. You did an awful thing to all of us."

"Yet you brought me along. You must trust me a little."

"I don't look at it that way. The way I see it, I'm taking you home."

She laughed. "No doubt I deserve that, but we're here now, and we have to set our differences aside and put the past behind us." She stood and offered her hand. "What do you say? Do you want to defeat Black Frost together or not?"

Grey Cloak groaned inside. Zanna was right. They needed to move on and work together. The fates of his friends and the rest of the world were on the line, and he needed all the help he could get.

He shook her hand. "No more surprises."

"Of course not."

"Give me your word as a Sky Rider."

"On my oath, I will not betray our cause."

Anya approached. She stared Zanna dead in the eye and said, "You'd better not, or I'll take your head from your shoulders." She walked away, following West deeper into the canyons.

"She'd make a fine wife for you one day," Zanna commented.

"You can't be serious. Anya?" He smirked as he watched the fair-haired Sky Rider move on. "We get along like oil and fire."

Streak wiggled free of the narrowing in the tunnel, flexed his wings, then pulled his twin tails around to his face. They were twisted together. "All right, very funny. Which one of you did this?"

Feather, Slick, and Slicer ventured through the gap. "Wasn't me," they all replied at once.

Streak shook his head. "If you can't trust your own brothers and sisters, who can you trust?"

Dyphestive tried to help Streak untie his tails.

"Thanks, brother, but I've got it." Streak unraveled his tails and bumped Dyphestive. "But maybe you can help me pay them back later."

West led the way, with Anya by his side. Grey Cloak and Zanna followed, and Dyphestive and the dragons brought up the rear. They made it to the first bridge crossing, leaned over, and peered down into the chasm that hosted all the other links.

Streak said, "We can save a lot of walking and fly down. Anyone care to climb aboard?"

"The sooner we start, the sooner we finish." Grey Cloak climbed onto Streak's back.

They dropped off the bridge and glided down to the bridge of skulls at the bottom. The others came soon after, with Zanna and Dyphestive on Feather.

West climbed off of Slicer and said, "Never rode a dragon before." He gave Slicer an awkward pat on the head. "Thanks."

Two urns filled with fire guarded the open entrance into a chamber full of skulls of all sizes. The largest were on the bottom, and the smallest skulls were on the top.

A doorway at the back of the chamber barred further passage. West stepped onto its stoop. "The Flaming Fence is on the other side of this door. There is no lock."

Grey Cloak eyed the entrance. His fellow Sky Riders gathered by his side, and he gave West a nod.

West pushed the doorway open, and a blast of heat rustled their hair and clothing. A great wall of flames waited for them on the other side.

Grey Cloak led the way through the door.

39

THE FLAMING FENCE stretched to the left and right as far as the eye could see and all the way to the top of the cavern ceiling.

Dyphestive approached the wall and stuck his fingers into the flames. He held his hand in there for the longest time, then when he pulled it out, it was smoking.

"Is it as hot as it looks?" Anya asked.

"Hotter," Dyphestive replied.

Anya shed her dragon armor. She stripped down to her shirt, trousers, boots, and sword belt. She tied her hair back and faced the wall. "Shall I go first?"

"I'm not so certain all of us need to go," Grey Cloak said.

"What do you mean?" Dyphestive asked. "I go if you go."

"Listen to me. I have the cloak and the Scarf of

Shadows and can slip into the Nether Realm undetected. It will allow me to locate our friends, the Dragon Helm, and the Star of Light. We'll be able to make a hasty escape, if all goes right."

"And if it doesn't?" Anya asked.

"Give me half a day. If I don't return, come after me."

"Half a day?" Dyphestive shook his head. "I'll give you a few hours, at best."

"This is a dangerous plan, but I agree with Grey Cloak," Zanna said. "He'll have the best chance to navigate the Nether Realm alone and unfettered by us."

"Boss, you can't go without us," Streak said. "You need us."

"I can do this. I've been preparing over a decade for this day." He started toward the flames. "I'll return, and I won't return alone." He took off the bandolier of vials and tossed it to Zanna. "In case you need it more than I do."

"Grey, no—" Dyphestive blurted.

Dyphestive's voice was smothered by the roar of the flames. Grey Cloak pressed farther into the wall of suffocating heat. He'd been through dragon fire, but its scorching flames didn't feel anything like the Flaming Fence. The fiery barrier penetrated his skin down to the bone, heating him from the inside out. He marched on, chin down. The agony forced a scream from his mouth.

Onward he went, one step at a time, fearing that his body and clothing would be consumed at any moment.

The flames nipped at him but didn't latch on. They searched for something to consume but didn't find it.

Turn back, the churning fires warned him. *Turn back before you perish.*

The heat sapped the strength from his limbs. His legs fell like boiling water. Each step was as agonizing as the next, but he trudged on and burst through.

He landed on his hands and knees, gasping. Steam rose from the Cloak of Legends. He crawled back to his feet.

I made it.

The Flaming Fence loomed behind him. He walked across a shelf of land and stopped at a rim overlooking an expansive underground plain that led to a vast city of decay.

And that must be the Nether Realm.

A screeching dragon flew his way.

Zooks!

He pulled the Scarf of Shadows over his nose and made his way down the grand staircase chiseled from rock.

A dragon rider flew overhead, leaning over the saddle. The dragon's head hung down, his burning eyes searching. Their gazes passed over Grey Cloak more than once as they circled the shelf.

The dragon screeched again, turned away, and resumed his course back to the city.

Grey Cloak had never seen the likes of either the dragon or the man. Their scales and skin had thickened and turned gray. The rider's armor was tarnished and rusted. Upon their grim faces were fiery expressions of bitterness and hunger for destruction.

So much for making new friends.

Grey Cloak moved down the stairs and across the plains toward the Nether Realm city. The distance between him and the Flaming Fence increased.

We're going to have one long run for it to make it back out of here.

The underground wasteland had many similarities to the Ruins of Thannis, yet it was broader and more expansive.

Disheveled people roamed the open fields, tending to strange plants that grew like stalks of corn. Man, dwarf, orc, and halfling were among them. Their distinct features had been altered— their gray skin was bumpy and warty, and most of them had white, thinning hair. Everyone's eyes burned with tiny flames within.

Grey Cloak avoided them and entered the city, where the citizens of the Nether Realm aimlessly roamed, their limbs heavy.

Dragons crossing the sky unleashed calls of frustration and turned loose raging gusts of flames.

Skreee!

Ten-foot-tall giants with shaggy beards and shabby clothing wandered the roads, shoving the smaller life forms out of the way.

A giant went out of his way to stomp a halfling crossing the street into goo.

Grey Cloak kept moving. He didn't touch anything or any person as he navigated through the massive town.

He spotted the great palace he'd seen in the Eye of the Sky Riders. *There it is.*

Dragons were perched on the immense building's eaves. Others were nestled in the columns of the domes.

Grey Cloak followed a group up the vast stairs that stretched from one end of the palace to the other. He entered the building between the columns.

The group appeared to be in a hurry, moving then traveling through the front entrance them moving to the back. Tilted paintings hung on the walls, their faded paint chipping and peeling away.

He didn't take time to gaze upon the chaotic scenes that marred the walls as he journeyed to the other side, where throngs of people were gathered on the stairs.

Their attention was fixed on a pale and slender giant of a man. He stood on a stage made of stone, high enough for all to see. He wore the Dragon Helm, and a woman lay at his feet.

Grey Cloak almost cried, "*Zora!*"

40

A FEW PEOPLE turned in Grey Cloak's direction. They stared for a moment and turned away.

He picked his way through the crowd and took the steps, nearing Zora.

Utlas spoke. "Look at my brethren! Our long-awaited day of triumph comes! Freedom will soon be ours! We will roam the lands above once more and take over the world!"

The people screamed at the top of their lungs. Their tongues curled out of their mouths, and their breath stank.

Grey Cloak pinched his nose.

Dirty chipmunks. Eat some ginger root or something.

The stench of the decaying people became overwhelming, so he focused on Zora. She sat on the slab of stone with a chain and a collar around her neck, her head down.

Grey Cloak's blood stirred.

Keep calm. Wait and see what happens.

With the chain in his grip, Utlas continued to speak. "Look at this little one. An interloper who came to steal our precious prize." He raised his fist. "The Helm of the Dragons!"

Dragons soared overhead, shooting streams of fire and roaring like thunder.

"I thought to destroy it," Utlas said, lowering his voice. "But I reconsidered. Why not keep it for ourselves? Why not rule the dragons above the surface as well as the ones below?"

The citizens cheered him on.

"After all, it came to us. It's a gift." Utlas tugged on Zora's chain. "We've received many gifts of late." He patted her head. "And I have this pretty little one to thank for it. Her and her friends." Crane's satchel hung over his shoulder, and he removed the Star of Light from it. "Ha-ha, I have it all! We have it all!"

Thousands of voices screamed all at once. The stones beneath them quaked.

Utlas laughed like a man gone mad.

Grey Cloak pressed closer to the stage and saw the weakness in Zora's eyes.

A ring of brutish armor-clad soldiers guarded the platform. Their spears had tips of fire that matched the burning in their eyes.

The Star of Light burned brightly in Utlas's palm. He gave a thin smile and put the star away. "The time has come to contemplate." He handed the end of the chain to one of his men. "Do not harm her. Don't let her run either." Utlas exited the stage and started up the stairs. The throng followed him. "Disperse, my fiends! I contemplate alone."

The sea of people following Utlas up the stairs departed into other quadrants of the building, and soon, the palace yard had cleared.

Grey Cloak slipped by the soldiers and stepped onto the large stage.

Zora sat cross-legged with her head down.

He crept up to her and whispered, "Zora."

She sat up.

"Listen to me. It's Grey Cloak. Not a ghost. I'm using the Scarf of Shadows."

Her chin quivered, and she started to turn.

"Don't draw attention to my presence. The dragons on the rooftops are watching."

She froze then slid her hand over the stone toward his voice. "I need a sign that it's you. Utlas tricks us all the time."

He placed his hand on hers.

Tears dripped from her eyes. "Rogues of Rodden. It's you!" she whispered. "I thought you were dead."

"Never doubt, unless you see a grave and a body. I'm as

alive and well as you." He squeezed her hand. "Where are the others?"

"Look behind us. They're dangling over the flames."

He spied Tatiana, Gorva, Beak, and Razor in the distance. They were floating on a cloudlike rock over an inverted bright and burning sky. His stomach sank. "This is a horrid place."

"Try living here for a while. Is Dyphestive alive?"

"He is well and waiting on the other side. So you're hitched to me now."

"You have a plan?"

"It's coming together. I'm going after the satchel. Tatiana needs the Star of Light to get all of you out."

"What about the Dragon Helm? You must retrieve it. Utlas was told to destroy it, but he wants to keep it. He's mad with power now."

"If that's the case, I can use it to my advantage, even if I have to kill him. Be strong a little longer, Zora. I'll return shortly."

"He's been gone too long," Anya said. She paced along the Flaming Fence, spinning her sword. "And I didn't come all this way to stand around and wait for something to happen."

"Aye, it bothers me too," Dyphestive said. "My brother does well on his own, but we work far better together."

"I agree. I think we've waited long enough." Zanna stood. "I'm going through."

"What about us?" Streak asked.

"I'm not sure that you can pass through the barrier. We don't even know if we'll survive," Zanna said. "Stay behind. We'll return, and we won't be alone either."

"I wasn't worried about you," Streak fired back. "But make sure nothing happens to the others."

"I will."

Dyphestive grabbed Anya and Zanna by the wrists and led the way into the flames. His skin heated but didn't burn. Fire invaded his blood and body. Hot energy spread through his entirety, burning away any darkness that lurked within.

He held his companions fast, towing them along through the conflagration of the wall.

They pulled free of the barrier and fell to their hands and knees. Smoke rose from them.

Anya rolled onto her back and said, "That was awful. I'd rather not go back through again."

"Agreed." Zanna fought her way to her feet and offered a hand to Dyphestive. "Are you well?"

He nodded. "It felt like a really warm bath. That's what I needed. Now what?"

Zanna removed potions from the bandolier. "We need to take these."

They eyed her.

"They won't turn you to stone." She twisted a cap off. "Here, I'll go first." She drank. Her skin turned ugly, gray, and bumpy, and her clothing became ragged. "If we're to survive, we'll need to blend in."

41

BISH

GEORGIO ELBOWED GOSSAMER. "TAKE A LOOK THERE."
Strange colors were bleeding through Dirklen and Magnolia's apartment window. "I smell a mage. What would they
need a mage for?"

"To find a way home," Gossamer replied.

"Oh yeah." Georgio shooed a fly away with his hat.
"Well, no one will be going home without us getting to
them first. They'll hang for what they did."

"Hang?"

"The citizens of Bone enjoy a hanging every once in a
while. It's entertaining, and it keeps them in line."

The thought of Dirklen and Magnolia hanging made
him a little squeamish. Both of them deserved to die for the
crimes they'd committed on Gapoli, but hanging sounded

like a brutal way to go. Not only that, but they were murderers on two worlds.

"I suppose you have to do what you have to do, but I need proof that I found them."

Georgio shrugged. "We'll gladly give you their heads to take back. Besides, if they don't have any kindred to claim them, we feed them to the hogs."

Gossamer gulped. He felt a hand on his shoulder.

"What are we going to do?" Datris asked. "If we're summoned back without proof, they'll surely kill us. But it will certainly be better for us if they're alive. I will stay on Bish if you wish to return with them. Perhaps you can find favor with them, and they'll come back for me."

"You make a good point, but that won't get us control of the Time Mural."

"Hold on," Georgio said. "You aren't taking them away from me. They killed some of my best men. Friends of mine. They aren't going anywhere until they're dead."

"I don't want to argue with you, Georgio, but our fate is on the line without them. We have to find a way that will satisfy both of us."

Georgio turned his attention across the street. "Well, you'd better think of something quickly. Because we aren't going to wait much longer before we storm the tavern."

The black carriage rolled in front of the Chimera's Claw and came to a stop, the black horses snorting. Once the driver set aside the reins, he climbed down from his bench.

The sounds of the carriage door opening and closing came from the other side of the vehicle. Then the driver climbed back into his seat and took up the reins, and with a snap of leather, the carriage started down the road.

Lefty Lightfoot popped up from the top of the carriage with a grin. He jumped down to the street and scurried into the barn. "That carriage reeked of expensive perfume and death." He fanned his long fingers in front of his nose. "Whew. No doubt she's a sorceress. And a cat in there tried to kill me."

"A cat?" Georgio asked.

"It was big. Like Octopus but with emerald eyes. Oh, and look at this." Lefty revealed a brass spy glass with runes on it. He put it to his eye and looked around. "Pretty marvelous, huh?"

"Did you find out any more about what she was doing here?" Gossamer asked.

Lefty shook his head. "The driver didn't have much to say. He sat on his bench the entire time, stooped over. He looks like the dead. Like Tonio."

Georgio's brown eyes widened. "Don't say that name."

Lefty walked away, holding the spy glass to his eye.

"Who's Tonio?" Datris asked.

Georgio frowned. His fingers caressed the handle of a well-crafted long sword. "No one."

Brak, standing on the other side of the stables, cleared his throat. He tipped his chin across the street.

Royal Lord Anton exited the Chimera and waited while a stable boy brought his horse around. The undersized man struggled to get into the saddle, but with a push from the boy, he swung his leg over and galloped away.

"We need to make our move," Georgio said. "Lefty, go around to the back. Tell them we're going in." He faced Gossamer and Datris. "Wait here. I'll bring them back so that you can have words with them. Perhaps you can use their gear as a trophy for your enemy. But I have a duty to uphold."

Gossamer nodded. "Understood. But they're dangerous."

"Oh, we know." Georgio pulled out his sword. "This time, we'll be ready for them and have the element of surprise."

"Please, try to subdue them. We need them."

"I can't promise that, but I'll do my best."

Georgio led Brak and a small group of his men across the street, and they quickly vanished into the tavern.

Aside from the beasts, Gossamer and Datris were alone in the stable, their gazes glued to the window.

"Do you think they'll kill them?" Datris asked. "Should we have stopped them?"

"Given our situation, I don't think we have much of a choice. We can only hope that whatever they do will work out in our favor."

"Perhaps we should have gone with them."

"It's too late now."

A horse-drawn carriage entered the other side of the stables. It was the same one the mage had departed in. The driver climbed out of his seat and opened the side doors.

Dirklen and Magnolia jumped out.

"Hello, Gossamer. What a surprise, meeting you here on the other side of another world."

Dirklen and Magnolia came forward with swords in hand then marched them to the carriage.

"Get in!" Dirklen commanded.

42

THE CARRIAGE WHEELS rattled over the cobblestone road. Dirklen and Magnolia made themselves comfortable in their plush leather seats but kept their daggers drawn.

"Care to tell us what's going on, Gossamer?" Dirklen asked.

"Black Frost sent us here to find you and return you home."

Dirklen arched an eyebrow. "You have an interesting way of going about it, using the City Watchmen who are hunting us."

"It's true," Gossamer admitted. "But we only hired them to help us find you. We were lost otherwise."

Dirklen leaned back in his cushiony seat and asked, "What do you think, sister? Are they telling the truth, or is this a lie?"

"I don't care either way, so long as they can take us out of this forsaken place." She reached across the carriage and grabbed Datris by his collar. "How does this work?"

Gossamer hated to admit it, but he had little choice, if he hoped to find any sort of mercy. "Whoever wears the collar will be summoned back."

"When?" she asked.

"I don't know when. Honzur knew he had to give us ample time to find you. He could summon us back at any time," Gossamer answered.

"Then what are we waiting for? Take those collars off and give them to us!" Dirklen demanded.

Gossamer nodded. "As you wish." He unfastened his collar. "I hope you'll find favor with us and come back. We have served Black Frost, as he commanded. And I believe Honzur spoiled Black Frost's favor with us."

"Honzur? What hand does he play in this?" Dirklen asked.

"He and Commander Covis control the Time Mural now."

Dirklen gave a puzzled look and beckoned with his hand. "Regardless, give me the collar."

The carriage rolled to a stop.

"What now?" Dirklen pounded on the ceiling. "Driver, take us to Lord Anton's castle with the utmost expediency."

Magnolia pushed her curtain aside and peeked through

the window. "I don't think we're going anywhere. We're surrounded by the City Watch."

"What?" Dirklen peered outside. "It's them! How?" He pushed his dagger against Gossamer's throat. "You did this! I don't know how you did it, but you did!"

"We had no idea," Gossamer said.

"Liar!"

Lefty Lightfoot's head hung down outside of the window. With a smile, he said, "No, he didn't have anything to do with it. We did."

"Who are you, little man?" Magnolia asked.

"Lefty Lightfoot, at your service. And if you put your blades away, I'll explain."

"I'm not putting anything away," Dirklen said.

Lefty shrugged. "Then it's probably best if I stay outside, because once you hear what I have to say, you're going to want to kill me. First, Gossamer and Datris have no idea what's going on. If they did, our plan would be lost." He stroked his goatee. "Where to start. Oh yes..." He snapped his fingers. "Lord Anton. That was your first slip."

"How so?" Dirklen asked.

Lefty continued, "He's a worm with a large mouth. Over dinner in a Royal house, he bragged to a close associate of mine about meeting a gorgeous woman with a scar on her cheek." Lefty glanced at Magnolia's face. "Ew, that is bad. But not so bad that it conceals your captivating beauty. Anyway, my associate Melegal sent word to us.

That was when the setup began. We picked out the sorceress Alania for Lord Anton. She's also a close associate of ours. He brought her straight to you and hatched the plan we fed her. She suggested you would slip away in the carriage and blindside Datris and Gossamer in the bar. Which did happen. And here we are. It's as simple as that. The two of you have been duped. And you might want to put those weapons down. It's time to surrender."

Dirklen glared at Magnolia. His nostrils flared.

"Don't blame this on me," she said. "How was I supposed to foresee what would happen?"

"If you'd never flirted with the man, it would never have happened!" Dirklen's eyes glossed over. "As for you and your friends, little halfling, if you think they're going to take us without a fight, you're wrong." Lightning danced in his eyes. "Get up, sister. It's time to take the refuse out!" He fired a bolt of energy from his dagger at Lefty.

The halfling leapt out of the way like a squirrel.

Dirklen spread his arms, and the roof and doors of the carriage blew off. Splinters and hunks of wood shot across the street. He and Magnolia rose from their seats.

"Look at this. Captain Georgio, isn't it?"

Georgio held the horses by the reins. "Give it up, Dirklen. You aren't going anywhere. Trust me. You're surrounded, and we're more than ready this time."

Gossamer spotted several members of the City Watch

on the rooftops, aiming crossbows at the twins. He nudged Datris, who was looking at them as well.

"Your men had better be very good shots, because those little sticks they're shooting won't penetrate my dragon armor," Dirklen said.

"No, but they will penetrate that skull of yours." Georgio stared him down. "Are you going to surrender?"

"And let you hang me for murdering your people?" Dirklen shook his head. "I don't think that would be wise."

Georgio dropped his hand, and the click of a crossbow trigger sent a bolt streaking through the air.

Dirklen plucked the bolt out of the air, inches from his face. "Tsk. Tsk," he said with an evil grin. "I tried to warn you." The missile glowed, and he hurled it at Georgio. The bolt sank deep into Georgio's belly.

Georgio dropped to the street.

Dirklen laughed. "Kill them, Magnolia. Kill them all!"

43

CROSSBOW BOLTS RAINED DOWN from above and bounced off Dirklen and Magnolia's armor. Cords of energy shot from their fingertips, stretching over the rooftops and boring into the crossbowmen's bodies.

Flesh, hair, and clothing burned. Dirklen chortled as power blazed from his fingers.

Georgio ripped the bolt from his belly, stood, and drew his sword. "Stop killing my men, Dirklen!"

"Fine. I'll kill you instead!" Dirklen unleashed of a streak of lightning that blasted through Georgio's body and into the horses'.

Georgio screamed as he was knocked back down to his knees. "Stop doing that!"

"Never! I'm full of energy!" Dirklen fed more into the charging men.

Magnolia did the same, blasting their weapons apart.

The back end of the carriage started to rise.

"What's this?" Magnolia locked her eyes on Brak, who was standing behind the carriage. "The beast of a man is lifting us!"

Brak's face was a mask of concentration. He pushed the back wheels of the wagon over his head and flipped it onto its side.

Gossamer landed on top of Datris, and Dirklen crashed down on Magnolia.

All of them scrambled from underneath the wreckage.

Brak snatched Dirklen up as if he were a child. Then the mammoth of a man slammed Dirklen into the street and pummeled him with his fists, which were bigger than hams.

Magnolia shrieked and hammered her energy into Brak's backside.

Brak arched back as his clothes and flesh started to burn. He let out an inhuman growl.

Dirklen and Magnolia hemmed the man in and buried their energy deep into his flesh.

Brak's body spasmed and convulsed. He foamed at the mouth. "No!"

Georgio crawled toward Brak. "Do something!" he yelled at Gossamer.

Gossamer had magic that he hadn't tapped into on Bish. He raised his palms.

I have no idea what will work.

The triumph in the twins' eyes meant death and victory. They were burning Brak alive.

I must do something.

All of a sudden, Magnolia channeled her energy into Dirklen. Strands of white light pierced his armor. Dirklen's jaw dropped, and his eyes grew wide. "Betrayer! Have you gone mad?"

"I'm not doing it!" she shouted. "I can't control it!"

Dirklen snarled and sent his energy into his sister. "I will destroy you first!"

Lightning bolts formed a net around them as they fought like wild dogs gone mad. Their armor started to glow red hot.

"Stop it, Dirklen! Stop it!" Magnolia pleaded.

"You first!"

"I can't!"

A white-hot flash preceded an earsplitting explosion.

Bodies and carriage debris flew across the street.

Gossamer was rolled up against a broken trough with his clothing soaked in water.

Datris helped him to his feet. "Impressive. How did you turn one against the other?" he asked.

"I didn't."

Dirklen and Magnolia were lying in the road, but their chests were still rising and falling.

Georgio and Lefty stood over the twins, scratching their heads.

"What happened?" Georgio asked as he patted the smoky holes in his clothing.

Lefty shrugged. "They went out of their skulls."

"They might have had a little help with that."

Everyone turned toward the sound of the newcomer's voice. Melegal walked down a storefront's steps, twirling his floppy gray hat. He dabbed a handkerchief under his nose.

"I should have known," Georgio said. "I have to admit I'm thankful this time."

"Thankful for what?" Gossamer asked.

Melegal put his hat on and said, "I have a special gift that allows me to control other people's gray matter."

"You might want to use it on Brak," Lefty said, "because I think he's about to explode."

Brak sat on his knees, growling and grumbling. The muscles in his arms kept pumping.

"If we can't control him, he might kill anyone he sees," Georgio warned Melegal as he started to step back. "Do something."

"I already have a headache. And can't you see my nose is bleeding? You can always run."

Brak picked up Dirklen's sword, which had fallen to the street, and started to rise. Only the whites of his eyes were showing.

Georgio shoved Lefty forward. "Talk to him. He listens to you."

"Me? You talk to him. I'll get him some food."

Brak's throat rumbled like a hungry wolf's.

Twinkling lights caught Gossamer's eyes. He'd lost his collar, but he found it near Georgio's feet. The gemstones started to pulse. "Datris, look!"

Georgio picked up the collar. "What's going on with this?"

"They're summoning us back," Gossamer said. "We're certain to be slaughtered."

"Not if I can help it. I have an idea." Lefty pulled out the extra collar he'd stolen from Gossamer. He ducked under Brak's swing then snapped the collar around Brak's ankle. "Stay clear and let him do the dirty work!" he yelled from behind Brak's legs.

"No, wait!" Gossamer said as he reached for the collar in Georgio's hand.

Georgio, Brak, and Datris started to fade, and in a wink of an eye, they were gone.

Gossamer's head drooped. "Oh no. I'll be trapped here."

Melegal placed his hand on Gossamer's shoulder and said, "We're all trapped here. Don't worry. You won't get used to it."

Lefty moved to the spot where Brak had disappeared. His mouth formed an *O*. "Now, that is what I call magic."

He snapped his fingers. "Blink, and they were gone. It reminds me of a little somebody."

"Don't even bring it up. The last thing we need is for that imp to show up." Melegal peered at the spot where Georgio had been standing. "But on a good note, at least Georgio is gone."

"What happens now, Gossamer? Will they be back?" Lefty asked.

"I have no idea. I'm the only other one that can control the portal."

44

WIZARD WATCH

HONZUR STOOD over the Pedestal of Power and adjusted the twinkling stones within. "The time to summon Gossamer and Datris has come, Commander Covis. Are your men ready?"

Commander Covis stood in front of his throne with a bored expression and said, "Aye, but I don't see the need for soldiers. The elves are harmless."

Black Guard stood inside the chamber, carrying spears. Four stood in front of the Time Mural, and two guarded the pedestal.

"It's always wise to take precautions. After all, I will be wrapped up in controlling the portal. We don't want to allow for any surprises."

Covis scoffed. "I'll be surprised if they come back at all. And I wouldn't be disappointed if Dirklen and Magnolia didn't make it. I never understood why Black Frost was so approving of them. I'm every bit as formidable."

"Perhaps this will be your time to prove yourself, if they don't make it back."

"If they don't and Gossamer and Datris do, what shall we do with them?"

"That's why I brought the Black Guard," Honzur replied. "So they can kill them."

"I could handle the matter myself," Covis grumbled.

"No need to soil your hands if you don't have to. That's what our servants are for." Honzur adjusted a few more stones and placed his hands on the rim of the bowl. "There. Now I shall reopen the portal."

The gemstones embedded in the base of the pedestal and the Time Mural archway sparked with life. They pulsated like beating hearts and cast a myriad of colors throughout the chamber.

Commander Covis came down the stairs. "Black Guard, ready spears," he said. He tightened his grip on his sword and sneered. "Do not hesitate to strike on my order."

The stones inside the mural turned into a sheet of black, then a sea of a rough wasteland under a bright-blue sky appeared. Air like the hot breath of a giant filtered into the room, stirring Covis's stringy hair.

Bathed in sweat and panting, Honzur leaned hard on the pedestal and gripped the edges.

Datris appeared in front of the mural with a confused

expression. He blinked, and a rugged brute of a man appeared a moment later, holding a collar.

"What treachery is this, Datris?" Honzur demanded. "Who is this? Where are Gossamer and the twins?"

Datris steadied himself and said, "I can explain."

"Don't test me with your tiresome explanations! Commander Covis, kill this other-worlder and bring Datris to his knees!" Honzur ordered. "I'll torture the truth from him later!"

"Watch out, Georgio!" Datris warned him.

Georgio had his hands on his knees. He looked up in time to see two spearmen coming his way. He shifted left, dodging one spear, but took another one in the thigh. "Not again." He snaked out his long sword and chopped his first assailant down. A quick backhand strike dropped the other.

Commander Covis jumped down the last step and drew his blade. "This one can fight! An assassin! Black Guard, surround him and skewer him like a pig!"

A giant of a man appeared on the floor in front of the Time Mural, eyes ablaze. He chopped down a spearman with one stroke.

"Brak!" Datris yelled.

Commander Covis peered up at the monstrous man. "Thunderbolts! A challenge from a worthy foe!" He advanced on the man, and his sword blade charged with gleaming light. "Come. Fight like a true master, wild man!"

Brak went for Covis like a ravening wolf, bringing his sword down on him.

Covis blocked the strike with a resounding clang of sparks and mystic fire. His arms shook. "Ha! A strong beast you are but not strong—*urk!*"

Without warning, Brak's free hand fastened around Covis's neck. He lifted him off the floor and held him suspended in the air. Brak let out a bloodthirsty growl and sank his fingers deep into Covis's neck.

Red-faced and wide-eyed, Covis chopped hard at the giant of a man's arms. His sword fell from his hands, and he locked his fingers into Brak's arms. Coils of energy shot out of Covis's hands and burrowed into Brak.

Brak let out an angry scream, and his vise grip tightened. The hair on his head and arms started to smolder.

Covis's wizard fire started to fade. His brow no longer knitted in struggle but started to soften. The muscles in his arms gave, his body went limp, and the lights in his eyes went out.

"No!" Honzur shouted. His allies were being slaughtered. He unleashed a bolt of energy from the rings on his fingers, striking Brak in the back.

Brak spun around and roared. He flung Covis into Honzur and knocked the pedestal over. Gemstones scattered all over the floor. The image in the Time Mural faded back into a stone wall.

Honzur crawled from underneath Covis's body and

shoved it aside. Brak's shadow loomed over him. His big foot came down, and he stomped Honzur to death.

Georgio slew all of the Black Guard with his sword, save one who fled toward the door.

The Black Guard pushed the lever back, opening the slab door, then crawled through the gap in a desperate effort before Brak could grab him. Brak gave chase.

"Close the door back!" Georgio said as he wiped the blood from his sword on a dead man's back.

Datris gave him a funny look and asked, "Why? What about Brak?"

"You don't want him to come back here before he calms down. He'll kill us," Georgio replied.

"I see." Datris pushed the lever back and took a breath. "I don't want any part of that. Does it take him long to calm down?"

"He'll settle down once everything he's hunting is dead."

Datris surveyed the area. The Time Mural chamber had become a bloody battlefield. Bodies lay everywhere, and blood seeped between the stones in the floor.

Then he spotted the pedestal. "Oh no."

The bowl had been knocked over, and the gems were scattered all over the ground.

Georgio picked up a diamond. "What's the problem? It looks like you're rich."

Datris climbed onto the dais, where Honzur's broken body lay. He picked up the bowl and set it back on the pedestal. "The problem is that I don't have the ability to send you back home."

Georgio's jaw dropped. "Oh. That *is* a problem."

Dalsay appeared from the other side of a wall and said, "Perhaps I can help."

45

THE NETHER REALM

GREY CLOAK CAUGHT up with Utlas inside a study within the palace. The walls were blanketed with half-empty shelving. Cobwebs filled the nooks and crannies, and everything smelled of rot and decay.

Utlas sat behind a desk, staring at the Helm of the Dragons. His elongated hands caressed the myriad of dragon charms that made up the helm's surface. Hooked on the back of his chair was Crane's satchel. The Speaker of the Realm was alone.

It's only him and me. I like my odds.

The Scarf of Shadows's concealment worked perfectly, allowing him to creep inside the room and draw closer to his goal. He passed the shelves, aiming toward a place where he could easily snatch the helm and the satchel.

Let's see. I snatch the helm and satchel the moment he

blinks. All I need to do is get the Star of Light to Tatiana. Then run like a mad elf back through the Flaming Fence. Ha. I knew I'd think of something.

Utlas took a handkerchief out of the desk drawer and started to polish the helm. "Soon," he said in his resonant voice, "control of dragon-kind will be mine. Certainly Black Frost will understand, and if he doesn't, I shall use it against him."

How alarming. He's going to use our plan against Black Frost. How does that saying go? "My enemy's enemy is my ally." It would be perfect, but I'm going to take that helm for myself.

"Freedom. I can't wait to feel the wind in my hair and taste the salt of the seas." Utlas set aside the handkerchief and lifted the helm toward his face. "Perhaps I need to try the powers first."

No! I didn't come this far to watch you model our helmet, you abomination.

Grey Cloak sped across the room and jumped onto the table. He retained his invisibility, but the table legs scraped across the floor.

Utlas swung his gaze around to Grey Cloak. The wrinkles between his eyes deepened. "Who is that? Who's there?"

A hero must do what a hero must do.

Grey Cloak charged the Rod of Weapons, revealing himself, and punched the burning spear tip straight into

Utlas's heart. "Some call me Grey Cloak, but you can call me the Giant Slayer."

Utlas threw his body back against his chair swiping at Grey Cloak.

Grey Cloak buried the weapon deep, pushing through the evil giant and straight through the chair.

The Speaker of the Realm died with his head thrown back and his mouth hanging open.

"That wasn't the plan, but there was too much on the line." He doused the flame of the rod, grabbed the satchel, and picked up the helmet. He'd never assassinated a monster before.

What had to be done, had to be done. It was him or me. Him or all of us. Filthy giant. I have no remorse for you.

With use of the Scarf of Shadows gone, he concealed the helm in his cloak, raised his hood, closed the door behind him, and headed out of the study into the grand hall.

This ought to buy me some time.

He passed several people on his way to the back entrance and waited at the top of the stairs, crouching by the support columns.

At the bottom of the stairs, Zora remained sitting on the stage, surrounded by a host of well-armed guards. She spotted Grey Cloak and nodded.

This is going better than I thought. Now all I have to do is distract those guards and free Zora. Should be easy.

Inside, the domes' great iron bells started to ring.

What now?

The dragons perched on the roof of the palace spread their wings and took flight. They soared overhead and across the rooftops.

A man hurried out of the building with his hands cupped over his mouth, shouting, "The Speaker has been assaulted! To arms! We're under attack!"

Assaulted? Utlas should be dead. Grey Cloak looked back through the building's entrance.

Utlas stood in the hallway, slouched over and holding his chest. He was surrounded by his minions.

Zooks! I knew I should have cut off his head.

"You there! Get up!" the man making the announcement said. "To arms, I said! To arms."

Grey Cloak stood and answered the man, "Yes, I have two arms right here." He tossed his rod from one hand to the other. "And they're ready to go." He hit the man across the jaw with the Rod of Weapons, knocking him to the ground. He heard yelling way down the hall and caught a weak-eyed Utlas pointing at him and shouting. He smirked and waved.

The guards bristled around the stage, and Zora sat on her knees.

Grey Cloak dashed down the steps. He hit the courtyard and continued his sprint toward the guards. They lowered their spears and braced themselves. He stuck the butt of the Rod of Weapons in the ground, vaulted high above the men, and landed on the stage beside Zora. "Guess who's here to rescue you."

She took the satchel and put the strap over the shoulder. "Great, but who's going to rescue you from them?" She pointed up.

Roaring dragons circled in the sky.

The enemies in the palace poured through the doors, and the guards surrounding the stage climbed the steps.

Grey Cloak shrugged and said, "I have no idea."

46

Clang-Clang! Clang-Clang!

Warning bells echoed through the Nether Realm's streets. Many of the citizens dropped what they were doing and hurried toward the sound.

Dyphestive, Anya, and Zanna traveled among the masses. They blended in well thanks to Zanna's potion, which gave them gargoyle-like skin.

"What do you suppose that is?" Dyphestive asked.

"If I were to venture a guess, follow the sound, and we'll find Grey Cloak," Zanna replied.

"Sounds about right," Anya commented.

Zanna took the lead. "Let's hurry."

They joined the stampede of the condemned rushing down the road. A palace of tremendous size came into view.

The ringing bells were inside its domes. People hurried up the stone staircase and poured into the building.

Zanna and Anya beat Dyphestive to the top of the stairs. He followed them inside, joining the flow of bodies moving through the broad girth of the hallways. Together, they pushed through the flock of rage-stricken faces and made it to the other side of the building.

A swelling sea of gruesome people had gathered around a large stage at the bottom of the stairs, where two people were fighting off many.

"It's Grey Cloak and Zora!" Dyphestive said. "We must help them!"

A man turned to Dyphestive and eyed him up and down. "Who are you who wants to help them?"

"I don't have time to explain." Dyphestive cocked his sword back and whacked the condemned man in the face. "I have a rescue to do."

"Look at the commotion over there," Razor said. He was the first one in the cage on his feet. "I need a sword. I need to be in there!"

Tatiana, Gorva, and Beak joined him.

"Do my eyes deceive me, or is that not Grey Cloak standing on the stage with Zora?" Tatiana asked.

Razor squinted. "Either that, or we're dead and dreaming." He raised his arms and waved. "Goy! Over here! Goy!"

"I thought he was dead," Beak commented.

"Never count anyone out, unless you've seen the body," Razor replied with a grin. "Especially him."

"He's come to rescue us. Dalsay must have gotten word to them," Tatiana added.

"Rescue us?" Beak rose on tiptoe. "They'll have a hard enough time rescuing themselves. Look at all of the condemned raining down on them. They need help!"

"Cowards!" Razor yelled. "If I had steel in hand, I'd take down half that army of fiends." He shouted at one of the dragons flying overhead. "Beast! Come down here and give us a lift!"

The dragon flew on, aiming for the backs of Dyphestive and Grey Cloak, who were fighting on the other side of the expanse.

Razor cupped his hands over his mouth and yelled, "Grey Cloak! Watch out!"

Grey Cloak turned the head of the Rod of Weapons into a two-bladed halberd and cut the arms off two attackers with one swing. He moved across the stage like a wild man, sweeping and chopping and keeping the enemy at bay.

Zora hid behind him. "Grey Cloak, we can't hold them off. What can I do?"

"I'll handle the masses. You take care of those dragons!"

"*What?*"

He kicked the Helm of Dragons to her. "Put it on. It has to do something!"

The mass of condemned breached the corner of the stage.

Grey Cloak grabbed a handful of coins from his pocket and flung them into the knot of raving soldiers.

A crescendo of concussive blasts knocked them off of the stage. *Boom! Boom! Boom! Boom! Boom!*

Grey Cloak pumped his weapon into the enemy at a feverish pace. The back of the stage was butted against the drop-off to the Flaming Fence. Hemmed in by the horde, they had nowhere to run. He sliced open a lizardman that rushed onto the stage.

Then the roar of the dragons came.

"Zora, we have company! You have to do something! Do it now!"

Zora shakily lowered the helm over her face. The steel and padding inside were cold and heavy. She searched for the dragons flying in the sky. "Go away!"

Nothing happened. Her body didn't ignite, and magic

didn't flow through her body. Her thoughts went stone-cold. "I can't do this. It won't work for me!"

"You can do it, Zora. If you don't, we're going to die!" Grey Cloak fired a wave of energy balls into the fiends. "Time is running out. What's the problem? Do I have to do everything for you?"

"No!" She glared at him then turned back to the dragons. She locked eyes with one of the flying monsters. "*Stop!*"

Her voice resounded in her mind like a hundred voices in one.

The grand dragon coming at her froze in midflight. Its momentum forced it into the ground, and it crushed dozens of bodies beneath its girth.

"Yes!" Grey Cloak shouted.

Zora felt like ten women in one. Energy surged through her, and she stood tall and proud. Her commanding voice carried around the cavern like crashing waves.

"*Dragons, heed my call! I am your commander! Turn your fires on the condemned! Burn them, one and all!*"

"Stop her!" Utlas called from the crowd. "Stop her before she wipes us out!"

A huge gargoyle of a man charged down the stage, swing his sword back and forth. He cut down his own kin. Two more followed him.

Grey Cloak tilted his head as the legions turned their attention on the dragons raining down fire. They started to scramble.

"Dyphestive?" There was no mistaking his brother's build, gargoyle skin or not. "Dyphestive! Ha!" He turned to Zora, whose eyes were rolled up in her head. "Don't kill Dyphestive. He's one of us!"

A dragon dropped down, blocking Dyphestive's path, and breathed out a tornado of fire, turning him into flames.

"No!" Grey Cloak yelled. His brother's screams rang in his ears. "No!"

47

DRAGONS RAINED down fire from the sky, engulfing the condemned in flames. They started fighting among themselves as they scrambled away from the wrath of the dragons. Fires burned everywhere, and thick smoke billowed through the cavern.

"Hold your positions!" Utlas commanded. "Giants! Attack the dragons!"

Men twice the height of ordinary men waded through the masses of people. A giant snatched a man from the ground and hurled him into the face of a diving dragon.

The dragon shrugged the man aside, then someone threw a spear under one of the dragon's wings. The dragon crashed into a group of people, and giants carrying iron clubs pummeled him senseless.

Grey Cloak fought on. Anya and Zanna fought in in gargoyle-like form, driving toward Dyphestive, who was swamped by surging bodies. Grey Cloak stuck his weapon into the chest of a condemned elf, hoisted him up, and flipped him over the ledge into the fiery bed of flames in the chasm.

"Zora!" he called. "Be careful! Get those dragons away from the stage! Dyphestive, Anya, and Zanna are down there!"

She was clutching the helmet, and her eyes were closed. She shouted back, "I'm trying!"

Zora had never felt such power. Dragon hearts beat inside her brain. Her blood pumped like it was spewing from a geyser. She controlled the dragons, all as one, but they fought back.

No, you don't. I'm in command here. Obey me!

The dragons formed a ring in the sky. One by one, they dove toward the earth and turned the fighting condemned into flames. The decaying society died by the score, but there were so many.

Don't let up! Burn them! Burn them all!

Dragons chased down fleeing citizens seeking shelter in the palace's great halls. Showing no mercy, they gave pursuit and burned the building inside and out.

The fire started to spread. Flames rose from the palace. Everything the dragon fire touched started to burn.

Zora controlled the dragons, but she'd lost control of herself, and chaos took over.

Using two swords at once, Anya carved her way through the masses like a whirlwind. Creatures fell before the wrath of blades. Sword tips skipped off her dragon armor. Anyone who attacked her was punished for it.

"Fall, my enemy! Fall and enjoy your long sleep!" She stepped over the dead, ducked, and dodged, thrusting her swords deep into the condemned's chests.

She hewed a path to Dyphestive, who was on his hands and knees. His skin was red and blistered, his clothing charred. "Dyphestive, you're alive!"

A crazy look in his eyes, he rose with sword in hand. He gazed upon his enemies as his blistered skin started to heal.

"Stop gawking and keep fighting, Anya!" Zanna shouted as she took down two condemned. "The skin of the gargoyle is resistant to flame." She pierced the heart of another fiend. "But not entirely."

Dyphestive cleaved a man in half with a two-handed stroke then cut off the leg of a nearby giant. In ones, twos, threes, and fours, the enemy started to fall against the trio's might.

"Anya! Zanna!" Grey Cloak yelled from the stage. "We need to gather the others and get out of here. Dyphestive, get up here! We'll fight together."

The threesome fought their way up to the stage, joining Grey Cloak and Zora.

"Where are the others?" Anya asked.

Grey Cloak pointed behind him. "There!"

Zanna asked, "Did you retrieve the Star of Light?"

"It's in Crane's satchel!" Grey Cloak fired a blast of energy balls, knocking the condemned off the stage. "What are you going to do?"

The fighters formed a wall around Zora and beat the surging enemy back.

"We need to get the star to Tatiana." Zanna opened the satchel, which was hanging from Zora's shoulder, and picked out the Star of Light. She waved her arms at the floating slab of rock in the distance and hurled the stone across the chasm.

"Are you out of your mind?" Grey Cloak asked. "What if they don't catch it?"

"If they don't, our mission is doomed."

"They threw something!" Razor said. He jockeyed against Gorva for position. "I have it!"

Gorva stretched her long arms over his. "I have it!"

The Star of Light sailed over them, and they turned.

Tatiana stood with her open palm up. The pink Star of Light hung suspended in the air. A slender smile formed on her lips, and she said, "*I* have it." The stone lowered into her palm, and she closed her fingers around it. "Let's go help our friends."

The floating slab sailed above the sea of flames toward the cliffs and the palace.

With a strong breeze in his face, Razor said, "Whoa, now we're moving! I can feel the steel in my hand and taste the blood in the air. Watch out, devils! Reginald the Razor is coming!"

A dragon turned their way and bore down on them with its wings beating like thunder.

"Oh. I didn't see that coming," Razor said.

THE HELM of the Dragons fed Zora's deepest, darkest ambitions. A fire came to life inside her. She turned it loose, using the dragons to wipe out everything that was evil.

Dragons dropped from the cavern sky, scooped up men in their talons, and threw them into the abyss. They destroyed everything in sight then turned on Talon.

Tatiana and the others who'd been caged ran toward Grey Cloak. A dragon was chasing them.

"Zora!" Grey Cloak called. "Turn that dragon away! It's going to kill them!"

Her eyes were glossed over. A shadowy essence of a dragon formed around her body, radiating colorful light.

He watched in horror as his comrades on the slab braced themselves for impact.

The dragon rammed the slab with its horns, flipping it to one side. Tatiana, Gorva, Beak, and Razor slid off the rock and plunged into the Flaming Fence.

"No!" Grey Cloak shook all over. He spun around and faced Zora. "What have you done? You killed them!" Using the Rod of Weapons like a club, he hit her in the head, knocking off the helm and scattering several dragon charms.

Zora's knees buckled, and she fell to the ground, clutching her head and moaning.

The rest of Talon was backed up to the ledge. The condemned came forward, pressing them back.

Grey Cloak and the others unleashed their fury.

"This is for Talon!" The Rod of Weapons burned like a bright star. Strings of energy blasted from the end and ripped through the hosts of the enemy. He reached deep, let loose his anger, and fed all he had into it. "*Die!*"

Utlas towered above his brethren. He started to grow and soon reached over thirty feet tall. His voice was like a raging storm. "*You sought to deceive me! You thought to destroy me! I will consume you all, one by one!*"

The Speaker of the Realm came closer, crushing his men beneath his feet. "*Who wishes to be devoured first?*"

Anya stepped forward and said, "Guess what, Utlas." She darkened her expression. "You're about to have a very bad day!" Her blade charged with energy, and a bolt blasted out, striking Utlas in the eyeball.

He staggered back, roaring.

Grey Cloak spotted a gap in the enemy ranks. He picked up Zora and slung her over his shoulder. "Everyone, follow me. Run!" He leaped off the stage and ran at full speed.

They bounded up the stairs, taking several steps at a time, and raced into the smoky hallways.

Grey Cloak held his breath. His eyes stung. Zora coughed.

They emerged on the other side then ran down the steps and into the streets, where chaos reigned among the people.

Driven mad by the Helm of the Dragons, the flying beasts continued their attacks on anything that moved. Burning buildings started to collapse. Rubble and dust spread across the roads.

Dyphestive caught up with Grey Cloak. He plowed over the enemy and hewed down anyone who stepped in his path.

Fleeing like deer, they departed the Nether Realm city and distanced themselves from the throng. They raced across the landscape with a raging horde charging after them, and they were still under the attack of the dragons.

"We're almost to the Flaming Fence. Hurry!" Grey Cloak urged his friends.

They ran over the next rise, where the stairway in the cliff to the Flaming Fence waited. The moment it came into view, Dyphestive slowed down.

Grey Cloak almost ran into his brother. "What is it?" He eyed the cliffs. "Oh."

The staircase leading to the Flaming Fence was crammed full of Nether Realm soldiers. They were lined up by the hundreds on the top of the ledge.

There was nowhere to go but up, and no one in Talon could fly.

"I don't suppose anyone else knows another way out of this place," Grey Cloak said.

"We could dig," Anya quipped.

"Now you choose to be funny," he replied.

The armies of the Nether Realm surrounded them in ranks ten rows deep.

Once again, Utlas walked through his army, crushing anyone that didn't move. A hole burned in the socket where his right eye had once been. From his great height, he glowered down at them. *"You would be wise to surrender. Or all of you will die!"*

Anya marched forward. "The same can be said of you, Utlas. We're quite formidable."

"Ha! Feast your eyes on my numbers. You don't stand a chance."

"We don't fear your armies, but you should fear us,

giant!" Anya yelled. "We will focus all of our attention on destroying you! And I promise it will be done!"

Utlas blanched. *"You will die either way!"*

"You will die first!" Anya answered.

"I see where you're going with this, but I don't think it's going to resolve our problem," Grey Cloak said.

"Perhaps not, but I'm not dying before he does," she replied.

Zanna moved in front of Anya and spread her arms. "Utlas, Speaker of the Realm, I offer a proposition."

Utlas tilted his head. *"I'm listening."*

"In exchange for their lives, I will remain and be your servant and slave."

"What?" Grey Cloak exclaimed. He grabbed Zanna's arm. "You can't do this. It's insanity."

"Grey Cloak, you must trust me. I trust you. I know you'll find a way out, for all of us." She pulled away. "Have faith."

Utlas rubbed his chin. *"Hm. I will accept your bargain on one condition. Leave the Helm of the Dragons behind as well."*

"Done!" Zanna agreed.

"Mother, no!"

"You can't do this, Mother," Grey Cloak argued. "We came all this way for the helm. And you have to return to the Time Mural so that you can save us."

"No," Zanna said, "you came all this way to save your friends. You must go. Find another way. You always do. I'll be fine." She hugged him. "I believe in you."

Grey Cloak teared up and swallowed the lump in his throat. "This isn't over. I will save you."

Zanna took the Helm of the Dragons from him, caressed his cheek, and replied, "I know." She sauntered over to Utlas, and a host of Nether Realm soldiers surrounded her. "Keep your oath, Utlas. Let my companions go."

"*Certainly,*" Utlas replied. "*Clear a path for our guests! But first...*" He pointed at Zanna, and the helm floated into his hand. With another gesture, coils of mystic energy ensnared Zanna's wrists and ankles, binding them together. *"I won't have any tricks, Zanna. You are mine now."*

The armies parted like the water in a great sea, clearing the way to the Flaming Fence.

With downcast eyes, the remaining members of Talon began their march. All of them looked back from time to time as the distance between them and the enemy increased.

Grey Cloak wiped his eyes. He took one last glance back.

I've failed. Not only did I fail to recover the helm, but my mother is a prisoner, and Tatiana, Gorva, Beak, and Razor are dead. This is all my fault.

They reached the base of the steps.

"Oh," Utlas's voice carried across his army. *"One more thing, fools! You aren't going anywhere! You are going to die! Nether Realmers, attack!"*

"Utlas, you broke your oath to me!" Zanna said. "To all of us!"

The giant shrugged. He asked in a normal voice, "What did you expect? After all, I'm evil. And you're the one who made a fool's deal." He checked his cracked and chipped nails. "Even a halfling would have done better than that."

He picked Zanna up and cradled her as if she were a doll. "Together, we will watch your son and all of his friends die. Heh-heh."

"Battle ring now!" Dyphestive ordered.

Grey Cloak wrapped Zora in the Cloak of Legends and set her down. "This will protect you," he said.

He joined Anya and Dyphestive, and they made a triangle around Zora.

The surrounding army advanced, outnumbering Talon a hundred to one.

"Come on, dogs! Who wants to taste my steel first?" Anya shouted.

Grey Cloak flipped his rod hand over hand. "Somehow I get the feeling you're looking forward to this."

"Of course," Anya replied. "Aren't you?"

"I know I am!" Dyphestive shouted. "It's thunder time!"

The cluster of evil soldiers advanced as one, but a powerful dragon roar stopped the army in their tracks. Every head tilted toward the fiery sky.

Four dragons in a diamond formation jetted across the horizon.

"Streak!" Grey Cloak yelled.

The dragons veered left and dove toward the ground.

"Let loose the dragons of war and cry mayhem!" Streak

cried. He unleashed his fire and rained down death on the condemned.

All four dragons landed, encircling Talon. Using their breath, they created a ring of fire, consuming the armies and driving them back.

"Boss, are you going to get on or stand there gawking? This is a rescue mission, you know," Streak said.

Feather picked up Zora. "I have this one. Now, let's get out of here!"

Grey Cloak climbed onto Streak's back, and Dyphestive slid into Slick's saddle. Anya jumped on Slicer.

The dragons spread their wings and vaulted into the skies.

"Streak, how did you get past the Flaming Fence?" Grey Cloak asked.

"We're heroes. So we took our chances." Streak flew higher, far out of harm's way. Rising above the cliffs with the others, he aimed for the Flaming Fence. "Brace yourself, brother. The fence is hotter than an oven on Thanksgiving."

"What?"

"It's hotter than a hot tub on New Year's Eve. Ah, never mind. Hang on!" Streak jetted toward the gargantuan wall of fire.

"No, Streak. Wait!" Grey Cloak said. "We have to rescue Zanna and the helm." He tugged on the reins, turning the dragon around.

Dyphestive shouted, "Brother, what are you doing? Come on!"

Grey Cloak turned and yelled back, "I'm going after Mother!"

Streak zeroed in on the pale, gigantic form of Utlas. "I take it that's the bad guy?"

"That's him."

Dyphestive and Slick caught up with Streak.

"You aren't doing this alone." Dyphestive's brow was knitted, and he shook his sword. "I'll take the giant's head off. You get Zanna."

"Done! I'll go low. You go high. Streak, you know what to do."

"You bet!"

Utlas's eyes widened on their approach, and he gnashed his teeth.

Dyphestive stood up in the saddle with the Iron Sword cocked over his shoulder. His eyes locked on the giant.

Grey Cloak had Zanna's full attention. He gave her a nod, and she nodded back.

Slick gained speed and pulled ahead.

The defiant Utlas didn't budge an inch. The corner of his mouth turned up in a smile.

Dyphestive unleashed a decapitating blow. The blade passed right through the giant's neck. *Swish!*

Utlas and Zanna faded out of sight, as if they'd never existed.

"What happened?" Streak asked. "Where did they go?"

Grey Cloak shook his head in disbelief. "They could be anywhere." He looked about but saw no sign of Zanna.

The Nether Realm dragons gathered in the sky and gave chase.

"What do we do now, brother?" Dyphestive yelled.

"We have no choice. We must flee. Streak, you know where to take us!"

They sped away toward the Flaming Fence with a host of dragons on their tails. The armies of the Nether Realms fired missile weapons. Arrows and bolts zipped by.

With his heart aching, Grey Cloak watched the wall of flame grow bigger and bigger. He knew the pain that came with it and closed his eyes.

This is going to hurt. But I deserve it.

They plunged into the flames. His screams were drowned out by the roar of fire.

50

STRONG HANDS LIFTED Grey Cloak into a sitting position. The scorching heat no longer seared his flesh. He was on the other side of the Flaming Fence, and a deep chill fell over him. He shivered.

"Looks like you're going to be fine," a man said in a rugged voice.

At first, Grey Cloak thought it was West, but the voice wasn't the same. He lifted his head, and his vision cleared. He recognized a familiar smile. "Razor."

"You sound surprised to see me," Razor replied.

"I saw you fall into the abyss."

Razor tipped his head over his shoulder at Tatiana. She was assisting Zora, who was wrapped in his cloak. "Tatiana had something to do with that. That dragon knocked the rock over, but she covered us in the star's shield." He wiggled his fingers over his head, forming a dome. "We popped out here." He squeezed Grey Cloak's shoulder. "That was a daring rescue. You saved us, and I thank you."

Dyphestive stepped behind Grey Cloak and hauled him to his feet. "Come on, brother. We did well today."

Grey Cloak had trouble believing his eyes. Tatiana, Gorva, and Beak were all fine. Zora appeared to be recovering. Razor wore his customary cocky smile, and Anya and West were tending to the dragons.

Grey Cloak allowed himself a small measure of happiness.

Then he remembered. "Zanna."

He faced the Flaming Fence. She was trapped on the other side, and they didn't have the Helm of the Dragons.

Dyphestive put his arm around him. "We can't do anything now, but we'll find a way."

"That's what she said." He stretched his fingers toward the flames. Guilt assailed him. He'd quipped about returning her home to the Flaming Fence. "I'm sorry, Mother."

Talon emerged outside of the Peaks of Ugrad and joined a jovial Crane, Tinison, and a host of dragons. Many hugs, hearty back slaps, and salutes followed.

A small hand locked around Grey Cloak's hand, warming it.

Zora asked, "Do you want your cloak back?"

"Do you want your scarf back?"

"I don't know. This cloak is very comfortable."

Grey Cloak hugged her tightly.

"I'm sorry about your mother and the helm. It's my fault," she said.

"Of course it isn't. We'll get her back. And the helm." He stared up at the frosty Peaks of Ugrad. "Somehow."

51

EPILOGUE – SAFE HAVEN

TALON and the dragons returned to the sanctuary hidden deep beneath the earth. After the long, harrowing journey, they rested.

Grey Cloak and Dyphestive joined Nath and Tatiana inside the armory at the Eye of the Sky Rider.

"Did you find her?" Grey Cloak asked.

Tatiana nodded. "Zanna is alive, but it's best that you don't see."

Grey Cloak clenched his fist. "Show me."

She nodded and passed a hand over the pedestal.

An image of fire formed. Great slabs of stone floated over the Flaming Fence.

Zanna was bound to a rotating rock by mystic chains attacked to her neck, wrists, and ankles.

"We have to go back for her. We need her," he said.

"We've been to the Nether Realm once. Certainly we can go back again. And we need the Helm of the Dragons. There is no other way to defeat Black Frost."

"Nath and I have been conversing," Tatiana said. "We believe Zanna did what she did for a reason. Though I admit I don't understand it. She knows we need her to return to the past through the Time Mural." She raised an eyebrow. "She is perplexing, to say the least. We have to remain on course to stop Black Frost."

Grey Cloak locked his fingers behind his neck and leaned back with a sigh. "How can we move forward if she doesn't return to the past? Zooks, I should have saved her! We need her and the helm to defeat Black Frost. He is too formidable. I don't see any other way to beat him."

Nath ran his long fingernails through his wispy beard and said, "I agree with Tatiana. We need to come up with another solution. Another weapon."

"What are we supposed to do? Build one?" Grey Cloak asked. "Black Frost is as big as a mountain. And it's only a matter of time before he finds us. We're on borrowed time."

Dalsay appeared out of nowhere. "Grey Cloak speaks truth. Time is pressing."

"Oh, now you show up. We could have used your help in the Nether Realm. If you'd come, we could have saved Zanna and the helm," Grey Cloak said.

"Believe me. Matters are more pressing at the Wizard Watch. The pedestal has been damaged, and we're struggling to rebuild it." Dalsay brushed against Tatiana. "It's good to see you again, my love."

"You as well," she said as her body passed through his.

"What? The portal is damaged? How did this happen?" Grey Cloak demanded.

"It's a long story," Dalsay said. He gave Tatiana a sincere look. "We need you to help with the pedestal so that we can bring Gossamer back through the portal."

"Where is he now?" she asked.

"Bish."

"Oh."

"Oh!" Grey Cloak said. "Zooks, is there any more devastating news you wish to share, Dalsay?"

"Easy, Grey," Dyphestive said. "We'll figure it out."

Dalsay continued, "And we have guests."

Grey Cloak eyed his brother, who in turn said, "Tell us they aren't underlings."

"No, men, like us. And we do have control of the Time Mural. Once it is repaired, it will give us a great advantage. But we must act quickly, before Black Frost discovers our deception."

"Is this the weapon you were talking about, Nath?" Dyphestive asked. "The Time Mural?"

Nath swept his long hair over his shoulder. "No. But with command of the Time Mural, I know where such a weapon can be found."

Dyphestive replied, "Let me guess. Bish."

Nath shook his head. "No, I'm talking about my home world. Nalzambor."

Will the Pedestal of Power be rebuilt in time?

Is there another weapon from another world that can destroy Black Frost?

Can Zanna be saved?

Find out in Ride the Sky: Dragon Wars Book 18! On Sale Now!

And don't forget to leave a review on Book 17. Thanks!
LINK

You can learn more about the strange world of Bish in the Darkslayer Omnibus. On Sale Now!

LINK

And if you haven't already, signup for my newsletter and grab 3 FREE books including the Dragon Wars Prequel.

WWW.DRAGONWARSBOOKS.COM

Teachers and Students, if you would like to order paperback copies for you library or classroom, email craig@thedarkslayer.com to receive a special discount.

Gear up in this Dragon Wars body armor enchanted with a +2 Coolness factor/+4 at Gaming Conventions. Sizes range from halfling (Small) to Ogre (XXL). LINK . www.society6.com

ABOUT THE AUTHOR

*Check me out on Bookbub and follow: HalloranOn-BookBub

*I'd love it if you would subscribe to my mailing list: www.craighalloran.com

*On Facebook, you can find me at The Darkslayer Report or Craig Halloran.

*Twitter, Twitter, Twitter. I am there, too: www.twitter.com/CraigHalloran

*And of course, you can always email me at craig@thedarkslayer.com

See my book lists below!

OTHER BOOKS

Craig Halloran resides with his family outside his hometown of Charleston, West Virginia. When he isn't entertaining mankind, he is seeking adventure, working out, or watching sports. To learn more about him, go to www.thedarkslayer.com.

Check out all my great stories...

Free Books
   The Red Citadel and the Sorcerer's Power
   The Darkslayer: Brutal Beginnings
   Nath Dragon—Quest for the Thunderstone

The Chronicles of Dragon Series 1 (10-book series)
   The Hero, the Sword and the Dragons (Book 1)

Dragon Bones and Tombstones (Book 2)

Terror at the Temple (Book 3)

Clutch of the Cleric (Book 4)

Hunt for the Hero (Book 5)

Siege at the Settlements (Book 6)

Strife in the Sky (Book 7)

Fight and the Fury (Book 8)

War in the Winds (Book 9)

Finale (Book 10)

Boxset 1-5

Boxset 6-10

Collector's Edition 1-10

Tail of the Dragon, The Chronicles of Dragon, Series 2 (10-book series)

Tail of the Dragon #1

Claws of the Dragon #2

Battle of the Dragon #3

Eyes of the Dragon #4

Flight of the Dragon #5

Trial of the Dragon #6

Judgement of the Dragon #7

Wrath of the Dragon #8

Power of the Dragon #9

Hour of the Dragon #10

Boxset 1-5

Boxset 6-10

Collector's Edition 1-10

The Odyssey of Nath Dragon Series (New Series) (Prequel to Chronicles of Dragon)
Exiled

Enslaved

Deadly

Hunted

Strife

The Darkslayer Series 1 (6-book series)
Wrath of the Royals (Book 1)

Blades in the Night (Book 2)

Underling Revenge (Book 3)

Danger and the Druid (Book 4)

Outrage in the Outlands (Book 5)

Chaos at the Castle (Book 6)

Boxset 1-3

Boxset 4-6

Omnibus 1-6

The Darkslayer: Bish and Bone, Series 2 (10-book series)
Bish and Bone (Book 1)

Black Blood (Book 2)

Red Death (Book 3)

Lethal Liaisons (Book 4)

Torment and Terror (Book 5)

Brigands and Badlands (Book 6)

War in the Wasteland (Book 7)

Slaughter in the Streets (Book 8)

Hunt of the Beast (Book 9)

The Battle for Bone (Book 10)

Boxset 1-5

Boxset 6-10

Bish and Bone Omnibus (Books 1-10)

CLASH OF HEROES: Nath Dragon meets The Darkslayer mini series

Book 1

Book 2

Book 3

The Henchmen Chronicles

The King's Henchmen

The King's Assassin

The King's Prisoner

The King's Conjurer

The King's Enemies

The King's Spies

The Gamma Earth Cycle

Escape from the Dominion

Flight from the Dominion

Prison of the Dominion

The Supernatural Bounty Hunter Files (10-book series)

Smoke Rising: Book 1

I Smell Smoke: Book 2

Where There's Smoke: Book 3

Smoke on the Water: Book 4

Smoke and Mirrors: Book 5

Up in Smoke: Book 6

Smoke Signals: Book 7

Holy Smoke: Book 8

Smoke Happens: Book 9

Smoke Out: Book 10

Boxset 1-5

Boxset 6-10

Collector's Edition 1-10

Zombie Impact Series

Zombie Day Care: Book 1

Zombie Rehab: Book 2

Zombie Warfare: Book 3

Boxset: Books 1-3

OTHER WORKS & NOVELLAS

The Red Citadel and the Sorcerer's Power

Made in the USA
Monee, IL
09 July 2021

73234347R00154